The Telling

To the Philgreens
"With tiny thanks!"

Guy E. Reams (signature)

TENNESSEE TINYS • BOOK 1

The Telling

GARY E. REAVIS SR.

TATE PUBLISHING
AND ENTERPRISES, LLC

The Telling
Copyright © 2012 by Gary E. Reavis, Sr. All rights reserved.

No part of this publication may be reproduced, stored in a retrieval system or transmitted in any way by any means, electronic, mechanical, photocopy, recording or otherwise without the prior permission of the author except as provided by USA copyright law.

Scriptures taken from the *Holy Bible, New International Version*®, NIV®. Copyright © 1973, 1978, 1984 by Biblica, Inc.™ Used by permission of Zondervan. All rights reserved worldwide. www.zondervan.com

This novel is a work of fiction. Names, descriptions, entities, and incidents included in the story are products of the author's imagination. Any resemblance to actual persons, events, and entities is entirely coincidental.

The opinions expressed by the author are not necessarily those of Tate Publishing, LLC.

Published by Tate Publishing & Enterprises, LLC
127 E. Trade Center Terrace | Mustang, Oklahoma 73064 USA
1.888.361.9473 | www.tatepublishing.com

Tate Publishing is committed to excellence in the publishing industry. The company reflects the philosophy established by the founders, based on Psalm 68:11,
"The Lord gave the word and great was the company of those who published it."

Book design copyright © 2012 by Tate Publishing, LLC. All rights reserved.
Cover design by Shawn Collins
Interior design by Christina Hicks

Published in the United States of America

ISBN: 978-1-61862-275-4
1. Fiction / Fairy Tales, Folk Tales, Legends & Mythology
2. Fiction / Coming of Age
12.01.13

Dedication

To all the teachers who work so hard to give us the tools we will need in life.
  I wish I had paid more attention in class.

Special Thanks

To Herb Hamilton, my brother, whose talent at painting pictures with words has been invaluable.

Acknowledgments

First, I want to thank my Lord and Savior, who guides me daily, for such an active imagination.

Thanks to my wife, who has always encouraged me in my many endeavors over the years.

To my daughter, Kasandra, who spent countless hours correcting my spelling and editing my grammar.

My children and grandchildren, who supported me and have always been my source of inspiration.

I thank those family and friends who took the time to read my manuscript and offer advice and support.

Grandfather's Trouble

Mrs. Morris's history classroom was packed with restless juniors who were not the least bit interested in world history. Conor O'Brien was one such junior. As Mrs. Morris lectured on and on about the Huns or the Romans or some other group of long-dead people, Conor wished his life was more exciting.

He was busy daydreaming about being a secret spy when his best friend, Brittany, kicked the back of his chair.

"It is evident, Conor, that Alexander the Great does not hold your attention. It seems that you're needed in the secretary's office. I'll deal with you later." Mrs. Morris did not joke around about history, so Conor was glad to have an excuse to leave.

Just as he stood to leave, the bell rung, and the rest of the class filed out behind him. Brittany ran to catch up to him. "Boy, you're in for it tomorrow," she teased. "Where were you anyway? You didn't even hear them call you over the intercom."

Conor just shrugged. "Daydreaming, I guess. That class is *so* boring."

"Well, I like it! I think history is interesting," she said.

"Yeah, you would, you're such a bookworm," he said as he gave a friendly shove and headed downstairs to the office.

When Conor transferred from his old school to this private school, Brittany was the only kid who would talk to him. They had a few classes together, and over the months, they had become

good friends. Brittany was seventeen years old, five feet, two inches, and very petite. She always wore her long, dark brown hair in a ponytail that swung from side to side when she walked. She chose her stylish wide-rimmed glasses to match the color of her hair. She was very smart and always positive about everything. Everywhere Conor went, she tagged along.

Changing school in the middle of the year was very hard for Conor. He still didn't understand why his grandfather insisted he go to a school clear out in California.

His grandparents had become very protective of him after he lost both his parents in a plane crash. Conor figured it was because he was their only grandchild. He loved his grandma and grandpa very much, so he had not put up much of a fuss over the move. He knew that getting a scholarship to this school was very rare. At first he didn't understand why he had to work after school, cleaning the cafeteria. But now he realized it helped to pay for his room and meals. It had taken awhile, but now he was pretty much settled in and had made a few good friends.

Conor was also seventeen, with blue eyes and dark-red hair that he always kept short and neatly combed. He was just shy of six feet. Even though he liked some sports, he never seemed to find time for them. Working on computers and making gadgets took up most of his after-school life.

Reaching the first floor, he walked down the hall to the principal's office. As he reached the receptionist's desk. He noticed that Betty was talking to one of the students. Betty was the student on duty today. She was a cute blonde, five-foot-four and one look at her beautiful smile would brighten anyone's day. But when she saw Conor, the smile that was there a moment ago disappeared.

"Hi, Conor, a messenger just brought this for you. I think it's a telegram? I didn't think people still used them. Why didn't they just call or text you?"

"They live sort of out in the woods and don't have a phone," he said.

"I hope it's not bad news," she said as she bit her lower lip.

Conor took the envelope and opened it slowly, hoping the same thing. Worry etched his face as he read the few words it held.

FAMILY EMERGENCY STOP COME HOME STOP GRANDPA STOP.

His heart felt like it was in his throat as he read the words again. Turning to Betty, he said, "I need to see Mr. Dougherty right now!"

She pointed to the principal's door and said, "Knock. He's by himself."

Conor knocked.

"Come in" was the reply from the other side.

He opened the door and stepped into the lavish office he had only been in once before in the year he had attended here. Crossing the floor, he stood in front of the principal's desk. Dougherty, who had been reading some papers, looked up, "Well, what is it?" He said with a scowl on his face. Dougherty was well over fifty, short with a receding hairline that had left the top of his head completely bald except for a little tuff of hair just above his forehead. When he scowled, the jowls on each side of his face puffed out, and it always reminded Conor of a Bulldog. Conor cleared his throat and said, "Sir, I just received this telegram from—"

"A telegram? Who sends telegrams these days?" Dougherty interrupted. "Who is it from?"

"It's from my grandpa, uh...my grandfather," Conor corrected himself and continued. "It just said family emergency and for me to come home."

"Home? Where was it again?" Dougherty asked smugly.

"Tennessee," Conor answered.

"Oh, yeah, the *sticks*!" Dougherty said, raising his voice angrily. "Is this some kind of a *joke*? Why didn't he just call?"

"They live off the beaten path, in a secluded area, and don't have a phone," Conor said, trying to control his own temper. "That's why the telegram."

Dougherty stared at him, the muscles in his jaw twitching, "This better not be some kind of prank just to get out of school for a day or two."

"No, sir," Conor said, and he left the office, trying not to slam the door. *What a jerk,* he thought to himself. Then his mind went back to the telegram, wondering what could be wrong.

Graybeard

Conor was able to catch a late flight from LA to Nashville. As the 757 headed for Tennessee, he sat looking out the window, wondering and worrying what this was all about. His grandfather would never have asked him to leave school and rush home like this unless he or Grandma was very sick or dying. God forbid! It could be anything; he just didn't know.

I hope and pray they're all right; they're all I have now that Mom and Dad are gone.

Thinking back, he remembered the only other time he had received an urgent message at school. The small plane his dad owned had disappeared from radar somewhere over Nevada. His parents were going out to California to visit some friends. The search had taken two days and ended when the wreckage was found with no survivors. His heart felt heavy as he thought of how much he missed them. And now, only a year later, something was wrong with his grandparents!

As the plane landed in Nashville at three in the morning, Conor rechecked the note in his travel packet that had been waiting for him at the ticket counter in LA. The note said a car and driver would be waiting for him at baggage pickup. Conor was to ask the driver how long he had been waiting. The correct answer would be "Since one fifteen."

When he finally got his luggage, he heard someone call his name. Turning around, he saw a man coming toward him. The man introduced himself. "Mr. O'Brien, my name is Ed Barns, and I will be your driver. I have been instructed to drive you to your grandparents' house and wait."

Conor, remembering his grandpa's instructions said, "Oh, hi, Ed, how long have you been waiting?"

"I got here a little early; I think it was around one fifteen."

As they merged onto Highway 40 out of Nashville, Ed looked in the rearview mirror to see a very tired young man fast asleep in the back seat.

Ed announced, "Mr. O'Brien, we have arrived."

Moments later the car pulls into the driveway. Grandpa was standing on the front porch. Conor leaped out of the car to find his grandpa smiling at him. "Hey, Conor, it sure is good to see you. How was the trip?" His grandfather was the mirror image of Conor, if you tagged on fifty years, turned his dark-red hair to white, and added a mustache and beard. He stood tall and straight for a man in his early seventies and had a smile that was contagious. He was wearing what he almost always wore: a flannel shirt and bib overalls, always clean and pressed, with lace-up boots.

"Grandpa, are you okay?" Conor said as he ran up the steps. "Where's Grandma? Is she okay? I got here as quick as I could. What's happened? You said emergency! Is she sick?"

"Whoa, Conor!" his Grandpa said, putting his hand on Conor's shoulder. "We're okay."

"Where's Grandma?" Conor asked again.

"She's in the kitchen, cooking up breakfast—bacon, eggs, and homemade biscuits and gravy, I think. All the things you like!" said Grandpa.

"*Breakfast*!" Conor half yelled. "You said this was an emergency. My principal thinks this is an emergency!"

"Well, this is an emergency, a life-changing emergency, and your principal can think whatever he wants. You can finish school here!" said Grandpa.

Conor stood there totally confused. "You're both okay, and I have to change schools again? Grandpa, what's going on?"

His grandfather pulled him to his side and hugged him then turned him to the front door and said, "Let's go to the kitchen, and we will explain everything. Before going inside, Grandpa nodded to Mr. Barns. "Come on in and have some breakfast. This is going to take awhile."

Entering the kitchen, Conor's nose was overcome by the heavenly smells of the morning feast that was being prepared. Upon seeing Conor, his grandma wiped her hands on her apron and wrapped her arms around his neck, giving him a hug and kiss on the cheek.

"Honey, I'm so glad you're here," she whispered. The past sixty-six years had been kind to his grandmother. Oh, she had gained a little weight, and her once-blond hair had turned silver, but she carried herself well, and the twinkle in her eyes was still there and always made him feel like he was home.

Grandpa and Conor took a seat at the breakfast nook, and before Conor could say a word, Grandma handed him a cup of coffee. "Thanks," he managed to get out before Grandpa started talking.

"Well, Conor, it's like this. We were hoping to wait a little longer to give you more time, but the accident with your folks has changed things."

"Changed things? What things?" Conor asked.

His Grandpa looked at him and said, "It's just that," and he paused with a sigh. "Well, we're getting too old to take care of the Tinys anymore."

Conor set there a moment. "The tiny what?" he asked.

"No, not the tiny what, the Tinys!" replied Grandpa.

"What?"

"Huh?"

"Okay, the small what?"

"The small what what?".

"Well, you said you're getting too old to take care of the small, okay, tinies."

"I didn't say small, I just said Tinys!"

"Okay, and I said tiny what?"

"Well, you know, the wee folk."

"The wee folk? What are *wee* folk?"

"Huh?"

"What?"

Just then Grandma, shaking her head, sat down next to Conor and took his hand. She looked over at her husband of forty-seven years and said, "Let me try and explain it to him, dear. You see, Conor, our family, going back four generations, has had a secret task to perform, to watch over some very special friends. Your grandpa and I have been the guardians now for over forty years, and your father was to take over this year. But now that he is gone, it…well, it has fallen to you to take charge."

With the last few words, tears had formed in her eyes, and she started to weep.

Conor put his arm around her and said, "Grandma, it'll be okay. I don't know what you're talking about, but it will be all right!"

Just then a small voice was heard coming from the counter top just behind Grandpa's head.

"I think maybe I should explain it to him," the voice said.

Conor looked from Grandma to Grandpa, then back to Grandma, wondering where the voice had come from. Then from behind the cookie jar stepped out the smallest man Conor had ever seen. There stood a tiny, little man no more than twelve inches tall with shoulder-length, wavy gray hair and matching beard that flowed down to his chest. He had dark-green eyes and a friendly smile and was dressed in a forest-green jacket with brown pants and a floppy hat.

Conor just sat there stunned as the tiny man walked across the counter to the edge and stood there smiling. He looked at Grandpa, and they exchanged winks!

"Conor," Grandpa said, "I would like to introduce you to my old and dear friend Mr. Michael O'Doul, known to all as Graybeard!"

Conor just sat there, mouth and eyes wide open, staring. Grandma nudged Conor with her elbow and said, "Mind your manners, dear."

Conor looked at her, then to Grandpa, then to Graybeard, and said, "Whoa…you said…I mean…whoa…tiny…I thought…"

Grandpa said, "Conor, calm down and say hi!"

Conor looked again at Grandpa and then back to Graybeard and said, "I'm so sorry. Hi. I mean it's just so…wow!"

Graybeard chuckled and said, "That's okay, lad, it takes a bit of getting used to, I suppose."

Then the little man stepped closer to Grandpa's shoulder and asked, "Grandpa, if I may?"

"Be my guest," Grandpa replied with a smile as he watched Conor's face.

The tiny man climbed onto his shoulder and down his arm to the tabletop, walked over to Conor, and extended his hand, saying, "I'm glad to meet you Conor O'Brien the Fifth!"

Conor reached across the table and took the tiny hand between his thumb and forefinger and shook gently.

"I'm glad to meet you, sir," Conor said with a big grin. "This is really something! You have got to be the smallest man in the world! Oh! I meant no offense by calling you small."

"None taken, lad. Actually, I'm quit tall among my people," Graybeard replied.

"Your people! How many of them are there?" asked Conor.

"First things first, my young friend. I'm not offended when you refer to us as small or tiny or anything like that. We call ourselves Tinys, and we call you folks Bigs. Now to answer your

question, there are four hundred and two of us here in Tennessee. About forty-five are children; they of course are smaller than me." Graybeard grinned at Conor. "We are proportionately correct for our size."

Conor thought for a moment then said, "You said in Tennessee—are there more of you somewhere else?"

Graybeard looked up at Grandpa and Grandma and nodded his head. "Yes, there are about a hundred or so still in Ireland."

"Ireland!" exclaimed Conor. Then he slowly said, "You're not....leprechauns, are you?"

"Well, yes and no!" said Graybeard. "No, we are not leprechauns, everyone knows there's no such thing as a leprechaun!" he said with a twinkle in his eye.

Conor shook his head and said, "I can't believe I asked that." Without even realizing it, Conor blurted out, "But how is this possible? Where did you come from? How and where do you live? I have so many questions!"

Graybeard smiled, took his hat off, reached up, and scratched his head then said, "The how we came to be will be told at the telling tomorrow. As for where we live, it's not far from here in the woods. We grow some of our food, but your grandparents supply a lot of it. You see, lad, we cannot live in your world as you do. We would be put on display or used for wrong doings by unscrupulous people, and we cannot allow that. We are just plain, God-fearing folks, like you, with a few small draw backs." Graybeard chuckled at his play on words.

Conor sat there a moment then said, "You said something about a telling. What is that?"

Grandpa broke in and said, "That's tomorrow, and it will explain a lot more too, but for now we need to eat and get back to Nashville and meet with Janet at her office."

"Yes, I need to be getting back to the village," Graybeard said. Then, turning to Conor, in a soft voice he said, "Lad, I know you

GARY E. REAVIS, SR.

are really confused, but the next two days will clear it all up. Take it one step at a time, and I will see you tomorrow."

With that Graybeard walked to the corner of the table and climbed over the edge, out of sight. Conor leaned over and watched as the tiny man climbed down the table leg. All the years he had been at his grandparent's home, he had never noticed that the pattern carved into the wood of the table legs made a perfect ladder for someone Graybeard's size.

When Graybeard reached the floor, he tipped his hat to Conor and walked behind the stove, out of sight. Conor turned and leaned over still further to look, and that's when he saw, for the first time, a small little door that when closed was almost invisible.

"Wow," was all he could say as he set back up.

Grandpa smiled, "You will start noticing a lot of things around here we have modified to help them get around."

Conor sat in silence for a moment. Then finally he asked, "Grandpa, you said I needed to change schools again, why?"

Grandpa thought for a moment. "You need to because we want you to be closer to us and the Tinys, now that you know about them. It will be better if you live here with us."

"I guess I understand, but I just made new friends at that school. Hey, wait, how will I get to school? Does the school bus come clear out here?"

"No, the bus doesn't come out here, but we will buy you a car."

"A car, wow, that would be great, but you and Grandma can't afford to be buying me a car, can you?"

"I guess we can afford it. After all, we do have access to a lot of money, and I mean a lot!"

"I get it; your leprechaun friends gave you a pot of *gold*!" joked Conor.

"You could say they did, but in a roundabout way!" Grandpa said. "You see, they arranged for your great-great-great-grandfather to get controlling interest in several very large companies. That Micro, whatever, company you thought your dad worked

for, we own it along with about a half dozen other big companies. I don't know all the ins and outs of it myself, but that's why we have to meet Janet at her office and get you to sign some papers."

"Janet who and sign what papers?" Conor asked.

"Janet Cook, she's our lawyer, confidant, and the CEO of the company, and when you sign the papers, you will have complete control of Hawk Industries. Well, you won't have complete control until your twenty-first birthday, but you will have some. You will have all the benefits and funds you will need to help keep the Tinys safe."

"Hawk Industries? That's one of the largest corporations in the US!" Conor almost yelled. "How can…?"

"Yep," Grandpa said. "You really have to try and keep up, Grandson," he added. Conor once again sat with his mouth wide open in total confusion.

After saying goodbye to Grandma and her wishing them God's speed, the two settled in the backseat of the town car for the return trip to Nashville. Grandpa tried to answer Conor's many questions about the Tinys, Janet, and Hawk Industries, but he always ended with, "After today and the telling tomorrow, it will all make more sense."

"Is the lawyer aware of the Tinys?"

"Well, I trust Janet as much as I trust you. I have told her about them, but she has never seen them," Grandpa said then added, "She thinks I'm kind of off my rocker!" He chuckled.

Conor sat quiet for a few moments then said, "Grandpa, you know I love and trust you in everything. But if what you say is going to happen at this lawyer's office today, I just wonder how in the world can I possibly handle anything as large as Hawk Industries."

His grandpa smiled, "Conor, how old are you?"

"I'm seventeen, you know that," replied Conor.

"And how have you handled your life so far?" Grandpa continued.

Conor thought for a while then said, "I've always tried to learn as much as I could, trust in the Lord, and make the best decisions I possibly can."

"That," said Grandpa, "is how you are going handle Hawk Industries. Besides, you still have a few years to learn the ropes before you have to take over, that is if you want to. As for me, when it became my turn, I decided to hire good people like Janet to do the day-to-day running of the company. You may choose to run things yourself, and if you do, I know Janet will be a good teacher."

It was just before noon when they turned into the parking lot of a large office building in downtown Nashville. A short walk across the parking lot and an elevator ride to the ninth floor brought them to the office of J.L.Cook, CEO—chief attorney. As they stepped through the main door, the receptionist smiled and pushed a button on the intercom, saying, "They have arrived, Ms. Cook."

Seconds later the door to her office opened, and there stood one of the most beautiful women that Conor had ever seen.. She looked to be in her early thirties and somehow very familiar. She smiled and walked up to Grandpa and gave him a big hug, saying, "Grandpa, it's so great to see you. I have all the forms prepared and ready for signing, like you requested."

As she stepped back, she looked at young Conor and continued, "And you must be Conor the Fifth. I've heard so much about you; I feel like I've known you forever," she said, shaking his hand.

"Please come in," she said, stepping aside and following them into her office.

Waiting on the couch was Brittany. "Brittany, what are you doing here?" Conor asked.

"Mom had me fly in from LA last night and asked me to come with her to the office today. What are you doing here?" They both look at Janet and Grandpa, who were standing there grinning.

Janet was the first to speak. "We thought that it was time for you two to find out a few things."

"What things? What's going on?" Brittany asked.

Janet pointed to the couch and chairs. "Let's all sit down, and we will explain." As they took a seat, she continued, "Conor after you lost your parents, you became your grandparent's sole surviving heir. Heir to a very large fortune, as the O'Brians are the largest stockholders of Hawk Industries. It was your grandfather's wish that you change schools to better protect you."

"Protect me, from what?"

Grandpa answered, "I haven't told you before, but we don't believe your parents' plane crash was an accident!"

"What?"

"We found evidence the fuel system was sabotaged," Janet answered.

"But, who would do that? Dad and Mom never hurt anyone! Why?" Conor asked with a tear in his eye.

Grandpa came over and put his arm around his grandson. "We don't know who or why. We only know it was not an accident. That's why we sent you to that private school in Los Angeles where Brittany was attending. We did ask her to keep an eye on you, and when you became friends we were both very pleased."

Conor thought about all this for a minute and then turned to Brittany and smiled. "So, you have been spying on me, huh?" he said with a big grin as he poked her in the ribs.

She tried to wiggle away from him. "Yes! But you never did anything that I could report back to mom about. You have such a dull life." She laughed.

He looked at her. "And this coming from the leader of the geek club!" Everyone laughs.

Conor had to read and signed the security forms, giving him access to Hawk's many company building and offices. Janet explained, "With your ID card, you are allowed to enter any building the company owns. Just remember you must be accompanied by an adult at all times. Do you understand?"

"Sure, I have the run of the place as long as I'm on a leash."

"I don't think you should take it that way, Conor. We have many government projects at Hawk, and there are rules we all have to follow," Janet pointed out.

"Sorry, I'm just kidding. I didn't mean to make you mad," Conor said.

"I apologize also. I'm afraid I take this job very seriously, maybe too serious at times."

Janet handed him a list of all the companies owned by Hawk Industries:

- Micro Technologies, manufactures computer chips
- Hawk Aeronautics, builds corporate jets
- Mason Toys, the third-largest toy manufactures in the world
- Reavis and Sons Commercial Buildings Inc., skyscrapers and shopping malls
- Morgan Oil and Minerals
- GRH Metals, leader in steel and aluminum manufacturing

Handing him a cell phone she said, "This has my office, home, and cell numbers; you can reach me anytime, day or night. Conor, I really love your grandfather and would do anything for him, and now my job is to help you. Oh, he's a bit strange, talking about little people and all that, but I know he is really a good man, and from what I've learned of you, it runs in the family."

"It sure does, darling. Are we done yet?" asked Grandpa.

"I do have an idea on how we can keep the kids in school together. If that's what they want?" Janet says.

Both of the kids say, "Yeah!"

"Okay, how about if we put you two in a private school right here in Nashville? We have a large home and Conor could stay with us. What do you two think?"

Brittany questioned, "You mean now? Let me get this straight. I have to change schools too! I have to quit living in LA and move back in with my mom! *Cool*! I'd love it!"

"Hey! When Grandpa buys me a car, we can ride to school in style."

"A car! Do I get a car?" Brittany asked as she looked at her mom.

"We'll see," Janet said. "So what do you think, Grandpa?"

"I think we might just be able to work something out," he replied with a grin on his face.

Conor felt as if the world had been lifted off his shoulders.

Grandpa asked, "We are done now, right?"

Grandpa got up from the couch and walked to the desk, picked up a pen, and was done in less than a minute. "We have to be heading back," he said.

"Conor, I mean it, call me for any help you need," Janet said.

She opened the door, and as Conor stepped out, he stopped and looked at Grandpa. "I would really like for Janet and Brittany to be with us tomorrow at the telling!"

"The telling?" questioned Janet.

Grandpa smiled and said, "You're the boss!"

"Okay! Janet, Brittany, be at Grandpa's house in the morning, and dress for the country," Conor said over his shoulder as they enter the elevator.

"What's the telling?" Janet still wanted to know. But they were gone. "I guess we'll find out tomorrow!"

24 GARY E. REAVIS, SR.

The Storm

In the village of the Tinys deep in the woods of Tennessee, two brothers had been arguing. It ended with one stomping out of the house.

A short time later, through the bedroom window, Eric had seen Bryan leaving the village earlier than usual. He noticed Bryan was carrying a pack and his bow. Eric quickly dressed and was out of the house, trying to catch up. He headed in the direction he had seen him going and was not long before he spotted him. "Bryan, wait up!" Eric yelled as he ran to catch up.

"What do you want?" Bryan asked as he turned to face his older brother. "Why don't you just leave me alone?"

"Hey, come on!" said Eric as he reached Bryan's side. "What's wrong? Where are you going?"

"I just want to get away," Bryan said hurtfully. "So just go back!"

"Not until I get some answers!" exclaimed Eric. "Are you still upset about last night's meeting?"

"Yeah, so!" said Bryan as he turned and headed deeper into the woods.

"Look, Bryan, you knew you weren't old enough when you asked. How did you expect them to react? You know the rules say you must be sixteen to become a scout. It's only seven months until your sixteenth birthday. That's not too long."

"It's not only seven months, and you know it! The counsel only picks new scouts once a year. That means I have to wait a whole year, Eric. A whole year! They could have let me start now. I can do everything a scout needs to do! I can hunt, fish, set traps,

scout, and I'm better with the bow than most. I can even hide and move in the forest better than you!"

"Hey, don't remind me. I don't want anyone to know my little brother is better than me in the woods," Eric said with a grin and a chuckle.

"So! You finally admit I'm better than you!" Bryan said, not returning Eric's laughter.

Again, Bryan turned away and continued walking.

"Bryan, wait! Why are you leaving? You know you don't have to!" Eric pleaded again.

Over his shoulder, Bryan remarked, "I will live in the forest. You know I can!"

"Boy! What a stubborn kid," Eric said to himself and then yelled to his brother, "Okay, but why don't you at least wait until after the storm?"

Bryan stopped short and turned to face his brother. "Storm?" he questioned as he looked skyward.

"Yes, storm," repeated Eric. "You can read the skies as well as I can. You just forget to look."

"I don't care if a storm is coming. I'll just hole up in a tree."

"A tree! Now that's a good idea!" Eric said sarcastically. "Just the perfect place to be in the middle of a thunder storm. You know, with lightning and all."

"Ha! Got you again," said Bryan. Grinning, he pointed to his brother. "I know lots of trees that have already been hit, so there! Lighting does not strike the same place twice!" With that he headed off into the forest.

Shaking his head, Eric started back to his house. Knowing he had to go after Bryan, he began his mental checklist of the gear he'd need. "It's going to be a long day," he said under his breath.

It started to rain as he neared his house.

"Eric!"

He turned to see who was calling and found Dina standing under the eaves of the house next door. He waved, and she motioned for him to come to her.

"Now what?" he mumbled to himself, knowing all along what she wanted. Dina had been following Bryan around like a lost puppy since they were five years old. Everyone knew they were a couple.

When he was close enough to hear her, Dina said, "Where is he going?" pointing in the direction Bryan had gone.

"Into the woods to pout!" Eric replied sarcastically.

"There's a storm coming. Why is he going into the forest in a storm? Why didn't you stop him?"

By now he could see the tears forming in her eyes. "He'll be okay," Eric said, trying to console her. "I tried to stop him, but you know how he gets when he's upset. Don't worry, I'm going after him."

"Please hurry!" she said, looking toward the woods.

"I will," replied Eric as he turned and ran inside his house.

By the time he had his gear together, the rain was coming down hard. The morning sky was growing darker by the minute. Standing on his porch while he adjusted his pack, he looked up at the threatening clouds; the way they rolled and turned was not a good sign. The storm had him very concerned. Heavy rain could mean flooding and possible high winds. He must find Bryan and bring him back; and he must do it quickly!

He moved to the side of the porch and picked up his star staff. As he lifted it, its weight reminded him of its purpose. The star staff had been designed by Gary, the village's fix-it man. He had come up with this new staff design after watching a porcupine defend its self from a much larger animal. The staff was made up of three separate shafts that were each pointed on both ends. They were connected at the center to swivel so that when in danger, the staff could be opened into a six-point, three-axis star. It worked as a great defense against large animals. When it was

open, it was big enough so that all one had to do was just hold onto the center and duck under it, and the points sticking out in three different directions provided a sharp protective shield. Shouldering the staff, Eric headed for the woods.

The area between the woods and the village was mostly cleared of grass and brush, but he stayed on the path anyway. The path was packed down from constant traffic and wouldn't muddy as fast as the rest of the area.

"Now, which way did he go?" Eric thought aloud.

"I think he's headed for the owl tree" came Dina's voice from behind a nearby tree.

"Where are you..." Eric tried to ask but was quickly cut off.

"That's his favorite place for thinking," she finished as she stepped out from her hiding place. She was dressed to travel and carried her pack as well.

Seeing her face, Eric abruptly said, "No! No way! You're not coming!"

As they neared the old owl tree, the rain and wind was getting worse, and Eric was starting to worry. "Dina," Eric yelled over the noise of the storm, "even if he isn't here, we better stay and wait out the storm."

"But—" she started to say.

"No buts! I let you come along because you said you would listen to me, and I say we hold up here!"

"Okay!" she said in a tired voice. She was used to traveling in the forest, but not in the middle of a storm, let alone one as bad as this. The rain and the wind had taken its toll, and she was soaked through. Even though she was concerned about Bryan, she knew he was totally at home in the forest, and he would be safe. She hoped.

Eric stopped at the base of the tree and waited for Dina to catch up. Looking around, he could see that the tree had at one

time been hit by lightning. It had caught on fire, and the inside had been burnt out. The years of weather had worn off most of the burnt wood. Birds and other creatures had made it their home from time to time. Signs of old nests were visible all around.

As he looked up to the top, he noticed this tree was taller than most of the others in the area. The branches at the top spread out like a ten-fingered hand reaching up into the sky. No leaves were left on any of its branches, and against the dark, stormy sky the giant hand looked very sinister.

"Come on, Dina, let's get inside!" He could see the opening at the base in between two of the larger roots. They climbed over the roots and entered the owl tree.

Once inside they noticed a big hole in the center that went all the way to the top and was allowing the rain to pour directly on them. Working their way around the debris, trying to find a sheltered spot, a field mouse scurried out, brushing past Dina. Screaming, she jumped back and lost her footing.

Eric, who was busy clearing a path, turned just in time to see the mouse disappear outside and Dina fall into a puddle.

Bryan, sitting all snug and dry, high above in an abandoned squirrel's nest heard the scream. Jumping up, he grabbed his bow and ran to the edge of the nest. He looked down and saw a mouse leaving the base of the tree. "That scream sounded like Dina," he said to himself. Then he heard what sounded like Eric, laughing.

"Hey, who's down there?" he yelled. Eric's head popped out, and he looked up to see his brother. "So there you are! It's wet down here. How do we get up there?" asked Eric.

"You climb up on the bark. Start just to the left of the hole for the best way." Bryan ducked back out of the rain. Just then, it struck him. "We!" he said. "We, who's the 'we' with Eric?"

Looking down again, he saw Dina climbing just in front of Eric. "Dina!" he yelled. "What are you doing here?" Then without waiting for Dina to answer, he yelled to Eric, "Why did you let her come?"

Dina and Eric reached the nest and climbed in. Immediately Dina went over to the side that was farthest away from Bryan, curled up into a ball, and tried to warm herself. She pulled her knees up, put her head down, and wrapped her arms around her knees.

Eric, knowing what was about to happen, wandered over to the other side and pretended to be looking for something in his gear. Meanwhile Bryan was just standing dumbfounded, looking from one side to the other. Nothing was said for almost five minutes.

Feeling the tension, Eric went over to the opening. He looked skyward and realized it had turned a dark gray-green. "Bryan!" he called. Looking up from checking his own gear, Bryan saw him motion to come over. Bryan could tell by the tone of his voice and the look on his face that something was terribly wrong. Going over to Eric, he looked outside. At first he looked down, but not seeing anything unusual, his eyes returned to his brother's face. This time, following Eric's eyes, he discovered what had Eric so disturbed.

Eric said, "Is there a cave nearby?"

Shaking his head, Bryan replied, "No, there are only trees around here."

"We must get out of this tree and find some better place to wait out the storm," Eric said.

From the tone of their voices, Dina instinctively realized something was not right. "What's wrong?" she asked Eric.

"You tell her," he said to Bryan.

"Tornado weather!" was all he managed to get out before Eric shouted.

"Funnel cloud!" he said, pointing the cloud out to Bryan.

"Is it on the ground?" Dina asked, rising to go to them.

"No, only about halfway down, but it's moving right toward us!" Eric said hastily.

As the funnel cloud moved closer, the wind picked up, and the trees begin swaying and bending. Branches broke loose and

moved through the air, and leaves and debris flew all around. Just then, a large furry head appeared at the opening. Eric and Bryan jumped back, immediately going into defensive postures.

"Blue Boy!" Bryan shouted as he recognized his friend, the large blue-gray squirrel. Blue, seeing Bryan, continued inside out of the wind and rain. Eric, meanwhile, still held his spear at the ready.

"It's okay, Eric! He's my friend!" Bryan reassured him. Bryan and Blue exchanged nods. Blue then looked at Eric cautiously and moved past him, going deeper into the nest. Turning his attention back to the storm, Eric moved to look outside.

"Here it comes!" yelled Eric. "Move back inside, and find something to hold onto!"

Bryan glanced around frantically and saw a place where the inside of the hollowed-out tree kind of formed a stump.

"Come here!" he shouted over the roar of the tornado. Pulling Dina over to it, he dug in his pack and pulled out a rope. "Eric, come on!" he yelled over his shoulder. Eric was still standing near the opening, watching the funnel move closer. "Eric! We can tie ourselves to this!" Bryan shouted as he started to wrap the rope around himself and Dina. Seeing what Bryan was doing, Eric moved to join them just as the owl tree began to turn with the wind. Looking up from tying the ends of the rope together, Bryan saw his brother knocked off his feet and slammed into a nearby wall. "*Eric!*" screamed Bryan helplessly.

With a great tearing noise, the top of the old owl tree, including the part they were hiding in, was torn from the rest of the tree. Spinning and rising, they were lifted high into the air, and their world became a tumbling nightmare.

Missing

Graybeard stood on the hill just west of the village. This was one of his favorite spots. From here he could see the entire village. He liked to start each day by coming up there to see that everything was in its place. He liked the morning just before the sun came up; the air was still and quiet. He could see lights coming on in the different homes as people were getting ready for another day. It was very peaceful. "How long will it stay this way?" he wondered aloud.

As he watched, he noticed the door of Gary's house open, spilling light onto the street. Gary came out and started walking toward him as he did most every morning. The village blacksmith and fix-it man, Gary was also an inventor. You could always find him in his shop at the back of their house, working on something. His love of things mechanical was only exceeded by his devotion to his lovely wife.

Graybeard nodded a good-morning to Gary as he came closer. Then he turned his attention back to the village, looking for his friend, the teacher. He should be leaving the schoolhouse about now, although he was sometimes late joining them on the hill. Graybeard looked closely at the schoolhouse to see if any lights were on. The teachers' quarters were in the rear of the building that served both as the school and the church.

"Ah," he said aloud, "he's up," as a light came on.

Gary, reaching the crest of the hill, said, "Good morning, my friend. Quite a storm we had last night!"

"Yes, it was, I even thought for a while there we might have a tornado!" replied Graybeard.

Just then Gary heard the sound of something crashing through the branches. Looking up, he saw a pinecone falling down toward them. He grabbed Graybeard up off his feet and dove quickly to one side. The pinecone made a crashing sound as it hit the ground exactly where they had been standing.

"Phew!" said Graybeard, "thank you for saving me. Are those pine cones getting bigger, or is it just me?"

"You're getting smaller," laughed Gary while helping Graybeard up. Gary turned to see where the pinecone had landed. "No need for thanking me. I was looking out for me too," Gary said with a slight grin on his face and a friendly pat to his companion's back. "That would have started our day off badly."

"Or ended it," replied Graybeard. As he straightened out his clothes, he said, "And today being the telling day."

"Ah, yes!" Gary exclaimed, remembering his telling day, a day of importance for the children. "So today you tell them about our origins."

"The ones that are old enough to know need to know now. It will help them understand why we are here in the forest and why we must remain here. I often worry about the young ones wondering too far or even wanting to leave. I don't want to imagine what would happen if the outside world found us."

"Will Grandpa be joining us?" asked Gary.

"Yes, and if all goes well with his grandson, we will be introducing him at the telling as well," Graybeard said.

Gary frowned as he asked his old friend, "What will we do if he turns down Grandpa's request?"

"We must trust in the Lord as we have always done. He has cared for us thus far, and I don't think he will stop doing so now," answered Graybeard.

"I do trust in Him, but it's hard not to worry, some!" remarked Gary as he noticed the door of the schoolhouse open. "Ah! Here comes Vaughn now. Let's ask if he has any ideas about what to do if things do not work as we plan."

Before Vaughn could even reach the bottom of the hill, Dina's mother ran up to him.

"Dina is missing!" she exclaimed.

"Missing?" asked Vaughn. "Missing? You mean she is not home? Maybe she is over at Bryan's. You know how she dotes on that boy," he said smiling. Vaughn was a teacher, historian, and scientist. He was constantly looking for new things to learn and was a member of the village council.

"No! I checked with Bryan's mother. He and Eric are gone as well, and they did not sleep in their beds last night! She told me that their packs aren't there either. I went home and checked; Dina's pack is also gone! What could those kids be up to? Have they run away?"

Graybeard and Gary noticed that something was wrong and came down from the hill to see. "What is it? What is wrong?" asked Graybeard.

"Dina, Bryan, and Eric are gone, and Ann thinks they have run away," explained Vaughn.

By now Ann was crying. "Where could they go?"

Graybeard put his arm around her shoulders and said, "Now, now, I can't believe they would do such a foolish thing as to run away. I bet they just went hiking in the woods and got caught in last night's storm. They are probably held up in some cave or tree. They will be back soon. Let's split up and ask around to see if anyone in the village knows where they went."

Gary stopped by Kasandra's house to see what she might know. He knocked, but there was no answer. "She must be out early making a house call," he said to himself. "I'll go back home and check with Lois." As he headed down the street, he saw Kasandra heading for his house. "Hey, Kas!" he yelled, and she turned to see who was calling her. The village healer seemed preoccupied with getting her long, blonde hair tied back in a ponytail and deep in thought. He could see the pockets of her coat all filled with this morning's herbs and cures she was just out gathering.

Having just turned thirty and raising her young daughter on her own, she was the youngest widow in the village.

"Oh, hi, brother, and what are you up to this morning?"

"It's some of the teenagers—Ann's girl, Dina, and the brothers Eric and Bryan seem to be nowhere around," he answered. "Have you seen them?" he asked as they entered the house.

Lois looked up from her cooking and, seeing Kasandra, said, "Hi, Kas!" Then seeing the worried look on her husband's face, she stopped what she was doing and turned to ask, "What in the world is wrong?"

"We are missing three of our young people," Gary answered. "And I was just asking Sis if she had seen anything."

After standing and thinking for a moment, Kasandra announced, "That's where I saw them!" She turned to face Gary. "It was last evening; I was just coming back to the village from gathering herbs. I saw Eric and Bryan near the woods. I could tell, even from a distance, they were arguing. After all these years of watching those two fight, I'm afraid I didn't pay them much attention. And with the storm already starting, I was hurrying to finish my rounds. Just as I was entering the house, I looked back and noticed Bryan heading toward the woods, and Eric was heading for home. I didn't think much of Bryan going into the woods. Surely he knew the storm was coming and would return before it hit. Later, as I was on my way to take some herbs to Lois, for Trey's arm, I saw Eric with his gear and staff entering the woods. Thinking this was a bit odd, I told Lois about it."

"Yes, I remember you did say that there was a storm coming, and you saw Bryan going into the woods, but we both really didn't think much of it at the time," Lois commented. Then she turned and set the pan she was stirring off the stove and headed for the door, "Come on"—she waved back at Gary and Kasandra—"let's go find out what this is all about." And out the door they went.

Heading down the main street of the village, they meet up with Ann, Dina's mother. She is crying as she said, "I have looked

for her everywhere. When I checked her room, I noticed her pack and walking stick are not there! Why would she leave? Where do you think she has gone?"

"Now, now," Lois said reassuringly as she wiped the tears from Ann's cheeks with a part of her apron, "I'm sure she didn't leave the village. She must be at someone's house, waiting out the storm."

"But I've looked everywhere and asked everyone. No one's seen her!" repeated Ann.

Just then Trey came walking up to them. "Seen who?" he asked.

"Dina's missing, and her mom cannot find her. Have you seen her?" Lois questioned Trey.

"Yeah! I saw her going into the woods near Bryan and Eric's house," commented Trey.

"When was that?" Dina's mother asked.

"Last night, just before the storm came," answered Trey

"Was she with anyone?"

"Nope."

"Did she have her pack?"

"Uh...yeah, maybe...she was carrying something. It could have been her pack."

"Did you see her come back to the village?"

"No, I went over to Conrad's house."

"Wait a minute!" Lois exclaimed. "Kasandra, you said you saw Bryan going into the forest just before the storm? We had better go check with Eric and Bryan's parents."

"Bryan!" Dina's mother said more to herself. "Dina was saying something yesterday about Bryan. Let's see... Oh! Something about him being upset with the council."

"The council?" wondered Lois.

"She was very upset about it," Ann said.

"Trey!" Lois called to him just as he was heading for his house. "Do you know anything about the meeting yesterday?"

"Nope" was his reply. "I'm off to work now."

"Gary," Lois said sadly, "I'm worried now! We need to find out what is going on and where these three teenagers are."

Nodding in agreement, Gary proclaimed, "Okay, let's go see Eric and Bryan's parents."

Graybeard and Vaughn had been checking with some of the villagers and now met up with the others as they arrived at the boys' house.

"No one has seen either of them since last night just before the storm hit," Graybeard announced as he joined the group.

"I think it's time we ask the scouts to go try to find them," Gary added.

"Yes! I'll send them right out," Graybeard said. Then turning to Dina's mother, he said, "As soon as we have found them or have any information, I will come and tell you."

"Thank you all for helping," she said as Lois and Kasandra took her to her house to wait.

Journey Home

The funnel never did touch the ground, but as it passed over the old owl tree, it got caught in its swirling winds. The force of the winds broke the top third of the tree off. It snapped right where lightning had done the most damage years ago. The branches at the top acted like an open umbrella, catching the wind and strong up-drafts, carrying the tree and its tiny passengers aloft.

The tree snapped, and it spun violently. The force picked Eric up and slammed him against the inside of the tree, causing him to hit his head, and knocked him unconscious. Blue Boy was also pinned to the wall. He gripped the wood with his claws and held on for all he could.

The spinning made the rope around Bryan and Dina feel like it was going to cut them in two. Dina screamed and fainted. Bryan was fighting to hold her up. The tree kept spinning and twirling as Bryan prayed, "Lord, help us!"

Just then the spinning started to slow, and Bryan felt as if they were falling. With a loud splash, the tree landed in a lake. Hitting the water trunk first with the branches overhead, the tree was driven partly under water. As it submerged, water rushed into the nest where the Tinys were.

As the water reached Eric, he came to only to find he was clinging onto a very wet squirrel. Eric shook his head, trying to clear his dazed and confused mind. "What's… Where… Got to find Bry…" The water rushed in, making it hard to see.

Just then the tree rolled out flat in the lake, and it floated on the surface. As it came up, it rolled over to where the opening to

the nest was facing straight up. When Blue saw the sky, he moved to climb out. Eric, still hanging on, rode out with him.

Bryan was struggling to get untied and to help Dina who was just coming too, and he yelled, "Hold your breath!" And then they were under water. The hole in the tree was filling fast, and as the rope dropped away, they both swam for the surface, gasping for air as they broke through. Looking around inside of the nest, Bryan turned to Dina. "Do you see Eric? I can't see him anywhere!" He dove down to search for his brother.

"Hey!" a voice from above Dina caused her to look up to see Eric peering into the nest.

"Eric!" exclaimed Dina. "You're all right!"

"Yeah, just a little groggy. Where's Bryan?"

Just then Bryan came to the surface. Dina pointed up, and when he saw his brother, he grinned from ear to ear. "Hiya, Bro!"

Eric, who was lying on his stomach looking through the hole in the tree and down into the nest, smiled and passed out. Bryan and Dina scramble out onto the floating tree. When they reached Eric, they rolled him onto his back. Opening his eyes he said, "What happened?"

"You passed out," explained Dina. "You must have hit your head when you were thrown around," she continued as she searched for injuries on his head. Finding a large lump on the right side, just behind his ear, she turned to Bryan. "He has a knot here and most likely a concussion to go with it. We will have to watch him for a while to make sure he stays awake."

"I'm okay!" Eric said as he started to sit up, wobbling as he did so.

"Yeah, sure you are," Bryan said as he pushed him back down. "I need to check out our situation, so just lay back and relax awhile."

"Okay," Eric said, and he gulped as a wave of nausea hit him.

Bryan looked around to find they were floating in a small lake about three hundred feet from the shore. Three hundred feet is

not far for a Big, but to a Tiny it is equal to eighteen hundred feet. He saw Blue up on the highest branch. Bryan moved to join him.

"Where are you going?" Dina asked.

"Just to get a better look around."

Eric, seeing what Bryan was going to do, said, "Be careful; don't make the tree roll over."

"Okay!" replied Bryan as he headed up a branch, moving slow and easy. After a few steps up, the tree started to roll.

"Hold it!" Eric shouted.

Bryan quickly moved back down. With each step back, the tree righted itself. Blue scurried down from his perch and stopped on the trunk, turned to his friend, and chattered at Bryan loudly. Moving carefully, the worried squirrel went to the other end of their floating prison.

"What was that all about?" questioned Eric.

"He was scolding me," explained Bryan, "for rocking the boat." He smiled and shrugged his shoulders.

"Well, you had it coming," Dina said.

"Okay! Okay! I'll take it easy!"

This time Bryan moved up the branch slower and stopped every few inches and tested for any signs of roll. Finally, he made it up to the highest point he could. Looking around he saw they were slowly moving toward the shore.

"We are being blown to the shore," he told the others. Climbing back down, he told them the bad news. "I took a good look around, and I don't recognize anything."

Eric thought for a minute and asked, "Do you remember which way we were carried?"

Bryan, thinking back to the time just before the funnel hit, "...I think the clouds were moving northeast."

"Northeast?" asked Eric.

"Yes."

"That's not good," Eric said with a sigh. "We could be very close to a town, and that means Bigs. We must be careful, *very* careful!" Holding his head and thinking out loud, Eric started mumbling, "My head hurts like blazes. I probably have a concussion. We are far from home, lost, and too close to a Bigs' town. How am I going to get these kids home safely?"

Just then bubbles came out of the end of the log where the tree broke off. Blue scampered past them, heading up into the branches. They each looked at Blue, puzzled, and then where the bubbles were forming. Just as the trunk started to sink, Bryan yelled, "Run for the branches!" as he and Dina grabbed Eric to help him up.

"I'm okay!" he said and shook lose their hold only to weave, stumble, and almost fall into the lake. Again, they grabbed him and lead him up to the branches. By the time they had climbed up on a branch, the tree trunk had sunk so far only a foot of the branches were sticking out of the water.

"Now what's wrong?" Eric said as he adjusted the star staff, which was secured to his back. Looking over at Blue, who was chattering like crazy with his fur standing straight up, Bryan looked in the direction that Blue was looking.

"I don't see anything," he said. Climbing up to where his friend was, he again took a look at the shore they were drifting toward.

"Dog, dog!" He shouted! To the Tinys, that are only twelve inches tall, a big dog like a German Sheppard is something to avoid, and avoid at all costs.

Eric was on his feet, steadying himself by holding onto a nearby branch. Dina moved closer to Bryan, and Blue was still chattering.

"Has he seen us?" asked Eric.

"I don't know," Bryan replied. "I'll go back up and see."

"Go very slowly this time, and maybe he will not see us. If he hasn't already," Eric stated.

"Okay!" Bryan said over his shoulder as he moved to climb the branch again.

"Bryan! Be careful" Dina said, not wanting him to go any higher.

Bryan climbed slowly up the side of the branch that was away from the shore in hopes that he wouldn't be seen. But with all the noise Blue was making, he didn't hold up very much hope. *Maybe,* he thought to himself, *maybe the dog will just see Blue and no one else.* He reached a place on a branch where he was at the same height as Blue. As he slowly peeked around, he saw the dog looking their way. The dog barked at the squirrel, turned, and ran into the underbrush.

"He ran off!" he told the others. "I don't think he saw us, only Blue."

By this time they had drifted close to shore. The tree stopped moving when the submerged trunk hit the bottom.

Dina, looking around and seeing it was too far to shore to swim, asked, "How are we going to get to the bank?"

You see, Tinys don't like to swim where they don't know the size of the fish or turtles that might be in the water. When you're only twelve inches tall, you could become fish food if you're not careful.

Eric had been studying their situation, and he noticed that some of the branches reached the bank, but they were way too far off the ground for them to drop from.

"Okay! I think I know how we can get to shore," he said as he began climbing out on a limb. "Follow me."

"Wait a minute, Eric!" Bryan said. "We can't drop from up there."

"I know, but if we all go out to the end, I think our combined weight will cause the branch to lean over far enough for us to jump down."

"Oh! I got it. Sure, that should work," Bryan said as he helped Dina out onto the branch where Eric was almost to the end.

When all three of them were as far out on the limb as they could get, the tree still stood upright.

"Now what?" Dina said.

"Well, I thought it would work," replied Eric, still holding his aching head. "Let me think a minute."

They all set there on the end of the branch, trying to figure out how to get down, when Blue solved the problem. He simply came out to the end of their branch, and his added weight did the trick.

"Whoa, hang on!" cried Eric.

As the branch started to tip and move closer to the ground, Eric said, "We all have to jump at the same time! When I say go! Ready...go!"

All three Tinys dropped to the safety of the ground, but Blue stayed on the branch as it swung back up. As it passed close to some branches on another tree on the shore, Blue jumped and made it. He climbed up into the tree and disappeared in the leaves.

Bryan and Dina stood up and started brushing themselves off. Bryan looked around to see where Blue went. Not finding him, his attention returned to his companions. Dina noticed Eric still sitting on the ground, holding his head and weaving back and forth. She called to Bryan, "Bryan, Eric is hurting very bad. We've got to get him back home to the healer."

Bryan knelt down by his brother. "What's wrong, Eric?" he questioned.

"It's my head. That jump made it hurt even worse! I must rest...I'm so...sleepy."

"No!" shouted Dina. "He can't go to sleep with a head injury!"

"I know," Bryan said. "You've got to stay awake, bro! You know you can't sleep now."

"Yeah, I know," Eric said weakly, "but I'm so tired."

"Get him on his feet!" Dina commanded. They both helped him up and had to hold on to him because he was so dizzy. Eric tried to clear his head with a small shake.

"Bryan, keep heading southwest...move away from here fast."

Bryan took a bearing on the sun and turned facing the correct way.

"Grrrr!" Standing in their way, growling and showing his large teeth, was the dog.

Bryan quickly moved to shield Dina. Eric unfolded his star staff and positioned himself between Bryan, Dina, and the dog.

"Get under the star, Dina," Eric said quietly, fighting to stay standing while holding onto his star staff.

Having never seen a full-sized dog up close before, Dina was frozen in her tracks.

"Dina!" Bryan yelled as he turned to grab her arm, forcing her under the star staff.

The dog, hearing Bryan yell, stopped growling and cocked his head to listen. Eric noticed that the dog was wearing something around his neck.

"Bryan, he is wearing a name tag; he's tame!" Eric said, pointing to the collar. "Call out his name." He then slumped to the ground.

Bryan moved so he could see the tag. Just then, Blue jumped from the tree overhead and landed between the dog and the Tinys. The dog growled again. Blue arched his back and flipped his tail, challenging the dog. Bryan had to move to the right out from behind Blue's big, bushy tail so he could read the dog's name.

"Come on, Blue!" he said more to himself than the squirrel. "Hold still so I can see his name better!"

After moving back and forth a few times, he got a clear look. "Jack?" he said out loud. "What a name for a dog."

"Call out his name," Eric said weakly. "His name!"

Bryan ran to a spot closer to the dog than he really wanted to be and yelled, "Jack, no! Jack, no!"

The dog stopped growling and looked at Bryan. Bryan wanted to run but instead moved closer. As the dog lowered his head,

Bryan remembered how Blue liked to be scratched. "Good boy, Jack!" Bryan said.

By now the dog was sniffing him. Bryan reached up and scratched him gently near his ear.

Slurp! Bryan got licked. The force of the tongue nearly knocked him down, and he was wet from knees to shoulders. "He, he!"—he laughed—"He's friendly, all right. Good boy, Jack!"

Blue, seeing that the danger had passed, scampered into the woods.

Dina came over next to Bryan.

"I want to pet him!" she said. "But I don't want to get licked like you did."

Eric came up behind them walking slow and using his staff as extra support.

"You know, you could have wound up as his lunch!"

"I don't think so. He responded to my voice commands," Bryan said.

"Yeah!" Dina said, turning to look at Eric. That was her mistake. *Slurp!* She got sideswiped with a wet tongue. "Oh, yuck!" she let out. "I thought you said he was friendly!" she said as she punched Bryan in the shoulder like it was his fault "Yuck, yuck, yuck!"

Bryan and Eric both laughed.

"We need to get going." Eric ended the fun by saying, "We must get away from where the Bigs are."

"Okay," Bryan said as he scratched the dog's ear once more and started off into the woods. Dina and Eric followed.

The dog just sat there, cocking his head from side to side, watching them leave. High in the trees, Blue, who had been watching all this, followed in the same direction; only he took the high road, going from tree to tree.

They had been heading southwest toward where they assumed their little community was. As they moved through the woods and the hours passed, Eric was growing stronger and no longer

felt dizzy. His head was clearing, and now he was concerned about finding out just where they were and how much further they had to go. He stopped and asked, "Bryan, do you have any idea where we are?"

Bryan, who had been paying more attention to Dina than to their surroundings, stopped and looked around, but all he saw was the forest.

"No, I don't. I'll climb that tall tree over there and take a look around!"

"Okay!" Eric said, and he sat down on some grass to rest.

Bryan quickly climbed the tallest tree nearby, and as he reached the top branches, he first looked in the direction they were going and then all around.

"What can you see?" Eric shouted, but Bryan was too high up to hear him.

Dina, sitting down near Eric, said, "It's hot, and I'm getting thirsty!"

"Yes, me too" Eric replied. "We will need to find water soon!"

Bryan saw that they only had about one hundred yards of forest left before they come to a cornfield.

"There's a farmer's cornfield ahead; maybe we can find some corn that's ripe," he yelled down the hundred feet or so to the two that were on the ground, but they couldn't hear him. Just then he heard a noise coming from the way they came. He shouted as loud as he could, "Something is coming this way!"

Eric asked, "Huh?"

Bryan, seeing that his brother couldn't hear him, jumped off the branch he was on and fell twenty feet to catch a small branch. Then he jumped again and landed another twenty feet down. He screamed at the top of his lungs, "Something is coming this way!"

Eric looked up to find Bryan almost half way back down the tree.

Bryan pointed to the direction it was coming from, "I can't see, but it's moving very fast and making a lot of dust!" He tried

to tell Eric. Then he spotted it. What he saw was trouble, and it had four wheels! He yelled, "Get off the trail; it's a four wheeler and coming right for you!"

Seeing how the machine was able to drive right through big bushes and over small trees and rocks, Bryan warned, "*Get behind a big tree, fast!*"

Eric jumped up and grabbed Dina's hand and pulled her behind the nearest tree. Just in time for this four-wheeled demon to come crashing through the bushes and right over the area where they had been resting only a moment ago! The driver had so much dirt and mud on his goggles that he didn't even see them running! As he barely missed the tree they were behind, he cranked on the throttle and spun the tires, sending dirt, rocks, and grass flying right at the two Tinys. A large rock just missed Dina's head as she ducked down.

And then it was gone, and all you could see was a trail of dust and hear the roar of the engine fading away.

"Are you okay?" Bryan yelled as he started down.

"Wait! Yes, we're fine." Eric commanded, "Stay up there, and find a bearing that will get us out of here!"

"Oh! Right!" said Bryan, and he climbed back up and took out his compass and started looking around for landmarks he could recognize. Down on the ground, Eric helped Dina up. They both started wiping off the dirt that completely covered them. Bryan spotted a landmark he knew, and he looked down at them to see if Eric was looking up, but he was not. So Bryan found a pine-cone and dropped it near them.

Eric looked up at Bryan who was signaling him to come up. So Eric got about half way up the tree when Bryan yelled, "I can see the Jamestown Airport light!"

Eric stopped and asked, "Where is it?"

"About three miles to the west." Bryan pointed in that direction as he answered.

48   GARY E. REAVIS, SR.

Eric thought for a minute and then asked, "Can you see the runway?" thinking that if they could see it, they could take a bearing off of it, because it ran north and south.

"No! It's too far away and hidden by the trees and hills."

Bryan began to climb down when he heard an airplane overhead. He stopped and watched it as it passed over.

"Hey, wait, I see a plane!" he yelled as he kept looking at it. "I think it might be landing." He saw the landing gear come down, and he got excited!

"It is landing!" He quickly returned to the top of the tree and watched. As the plane landed, he was checking his compass. Finally he said, "I've got it!" and climbed down.

Once he was back on the ground, he pulled out his compass again, took a bearing, and then squatted down. Brushing aside some leaves, he started to draw a map of sorts on the ground.

"Okay! Here we are," he pointed to the X he had drawn, "and here is the airport." He pointed to a line. "So, we need to head this way, and by the end of the day, we should be here, home!"

It was hot and slow going through the farmer's fields. None of them liked being surrounded on all sides by corn stalks six-feet high. They could not see more than a few yards, except straight down a row. They did eat some ripe sweet corn along the way. After walking through the corn for nearly two hours, Bryan held up his fist for them to stop. He held his hand to one ear so he could hear better and slowly turned back and forth to try to locate whatever it was he had heard.

"What it is?" Dina asked.

"I'm not sure, but I think I heard a machine," Bryan answered.

"Which direction?" questioned Eric.

Bryan pointed out across the field to his left and slightly behind them. "I think it's over there."

Dina grabbed onto his arm. "Is it coming at us?" she asked in a shaky voice.

Bryan was still trying to get a fix on just where the sound was coming from. Now they were all trying to hear it! Bryan took Dina's hand from his arm and told her, "You stay here with Eric. I will go find out what it is and where it is headed!"

Eric held up his hand to stop Bryan. "No, wait! We shouldn't separate! You could get in trouble, and we wouldn't know it!"

Bryan ran off in the direction of the noise and over his shoulder said, "Who me? I never get into trouble!" Then he was gone and out of sight. The two of them just stood there, waiting.

Eric said, "I really hate it when he does that!" He smiled at Dina.

Bryan had run about sixty feet when he broke out into the clearing that had been made by the machine as it cut and picked the corn. All he could see was row after row of cut corn stalks. He looked down the edge of the row that was still standing, and what he saw frightened him to death! A giant combine was coming right at him! Its tires were huge and crushing the ground beneath them. On the front was an enormous blade that was sheering the corn stalks off just above the ground. He quickly turned around and ran back the way he came to warn the others. He feared that his companions were standing right in the middle of the machine's way. He tried to shout, but the machine was too close, and now the noise was very loud and getting louder. He ran as fast as he had ever run before, knowing he was crossing the very path of this behemoth! He tried to keep an eye on the ground for his tracks to make sure he was going back the way he came. His quick estimate of how wide a path the machine cut was about thirty feet. He saw that it was now dangerously close, and he was not sure he could make it past the area it was now cutting. All the noise, dust, and wind were only adding to his fear and dread. The ground was shaking and the noise deafening; the dust was now so thick he couldn't see or breathe. And then it happened, his foot hit a rock, and he fell. As he hit the ground, what little

air he had rushed from his lungs, and his mind screamed *Get up!* His heart was pounding; panic slammed into his mind. Just when he thought he wouldn't make it, a pair of small hands reached out and grabbed him and pulled him out of the way of the machine as it passed with a roar.

"Got you!" Eric shouted.

As the dust cleared and he caught his breath, Bryan said, "Thanks, brother, I thought that I was a goner for sure! We must get out of this field and fast!" he exclaimed. "It'll be coming back this way soon!"

"Okay! Lead the way," Eric said as he made sure Dina was right with them as they moved out of the corn and into another problem… Open ground!

Eric was quick to see that each of the rows of cut stalks was about thirty feet apart and that there was only open ground between each row.

"If we go this way, the driver of the machine will see us!" he said.

"Yes, I know, but we cannot go back in there!" Bryan said as he pointed to the standing corn.

Just then Dina shouted, "*Look!*" as she pointed at another machine off across the rows of cut corn stalks on the far side of the field. "That one is picking up the stalks and throwing them into that truck beside it!"

Bryan and Eric both looked at where she was pointing. Bryan again looked down the row they were standing near and saw the first machine coming back their way, cutting its next row of corn.

"We had better hide and fast!" Bryan said. And Eric, who had been watching the other machine, turned to see what Bryan was talking about.

Eric said, "We are going to get caught between these two machines if we don't get out of this field now!"

Dina, who had been looking at the row of cut stalks, said, "We should go over this row of stalks and hide from the cutting machine and then run along the row after it passes."

Eric and Bryan both yell, "Go!" And they climb over the stalks just in time to hide when the combine passed nearby.

They spent the rest of the day running and hiding until they finally got out of the field and back into the forest. Compared to the last few days, the rest of their trip home was a breeze.

The trio finally arrived back home after their long and hazardous journey, just in time for the telling day! All the families were greeting them and asking them what happened to them. They spent some time explaining about the storm and the trip back. Graybeard, upon hearing of how Bryan took charge when Eric was injured, asked Eric if he might speak to him in private.

They quietly slipped away from the crowd and go over to Graybeard's house. Once inside, Graybeard asked Eric to tell him about the storm and their trip home and not to leave anything out. Eric told him all he remembered, and after about an hour, Graybeard asked him, "Do you think Bryan is ready to be a scout? Or is he still too young?"

Eric knew that whatever he said would weigh heavy on the council's decision.

"Yes, I do think he's ready. After seeing him in a situation like we were in, he proved that!"

Graybeard thought for a minute and then said, "Very well then, that's what I will recommend to the council."

Telling Day

The sun was washing the last of the dawn's gray away when Janet pulled into the driveway of the O'Brien's home. She had been there many times on business and a few times had stayed the weekend just to visit. She always liked the early morning the best, when the forest was just waking up.

Conor came out the front door and down the steps. "Good morning," he said as they were getting out of her car. He smiled at the sight of them; they were both dressed in blue jeans, tee shirts, and tennis shoes. Brittany's mom looked not at all like the lawyer he had seen yesterday.

"It's really great that you're here," he continued. "Come on in. We're in the kitchen. Would you like some fresh coffee or a soft drink?"

"That sounds good," Janet replied with a smile, and into the house they went.

In the kitchen, Janet introduced Brittany to Grandma, and there were welcoming hugs and greetings They sat at the table with steam rising from the coffee cups and the two teens sipping on sodas. After a moment of awkward silence, Janet asked, "Okay, what's the telling?"

No one said anything for a moment. Conor cleared his throat and said, "Well, you know that Grandpa had mentioned the Tinys to you?"

"Yeah, remember that?" asked Grandpa, grinning.

Janet sat back in her chair and looked at Conor like he had big floppy ears and was wearing a top hat. Slowly she said, "Yes, what about it?"

"Well, that's what Brittany, you and I are going to find out today!" Conor announced with a big grin on his own face like that explained everything.

With a sigh, Grandma said, "Sweetheart," as she shook her head and covered Janet's hand with hers, "I know they both sound like idiots right now, but if you will just bear with us for a few more hours, it will all make sense."

Janet looked into her eyes and said, "Yes ma'am!" as she thought, *What's wrong with these people?* Then she silently prayed, *Lord, you know I love them. Please don't let them be completely nuts!*

After that, Conor talked about being up most of the night thinking about changing schools. Grandma asked Janet how she was doing. While she talked, she worked at filling a picnic basket. It wasn't long before Grandpa said, "Sun's up, and it's after six; time to go!"

"Where?" Conor and Janet both asked at the same time.

"We need to take a little walk; you didn't think the telling was going to be here, did you?" replied Grandpa. With that, they all went out the back door, across the back yard, and followed a path that lead into the woods. As they walked following Grandpa's lead, they moved in and around the trees and foliage. They had traveled for a little over a quarter of a mile in silence when Grandpa stopped and announced, "This is where we wait!"

There was a fallen tree beside the trail, so Grandma sat down her basket and took a seat with Janet, Brittany and Conor sitting next to her. Grandpa stood in front of them and explained, "Now, you are going to be the only three people, with the exception of Grandma and me, that the majority of the Tinys have ever seen. What I mean by that is the surprise, excitement, and, well, whatever feelings you are going to have will be the same for them."

Brittany, at this point, looked really nervous, so Conor reached out and took her hand in his. She squeezed it and held on tight without looking at him.

"There are things we must be careful about, like where we stand and move. We don't want to be hurting anyone!" Grandpa said then went on, "Don't talk too loud or yell. Oh! And don't interrupt while the telling is being done!"

Then Grandpa fell quiet as he rubbed his chin, trying to think of anything more.

Then a small voice said, "Old friend, since you have them scared already, can I play? Arrrrrrrr!" Graybeard yelled as he ran down the trail at them, waving his arms. Janet and Brittany screamed, Conor jumped, and Grandma laughed.

Grandpa just smiled as he announced, "Oh, yeah, I forgot to tell you they do love a good joke!"

When everyone had calmed down, Grandpa said, "Conor, would you like to do the introductions?"

"Yes." He turned to their guest and motioned to the little man. "Janet, Brittany, may I present Mr. Michael O'Doul known to all as Graybeard. He is the elder and leader of the Tinys. He is the only one I have met so far," he added.

Graybeard walked up to her and extended his hand, saying, "I'm so sorry, I just couldn't resist having a little fun at your expense. I have heard so much about you two and Conor I feel like you are family!"

Then he turned to Grandpa, saying, "You said they was pretty!" Then, glancing back at Janet and her daughter, he said, "My ladies, you are beautiful!" as he removed his hat with a flourish and bowed to them.

Janet blushed and then, staring down at the little man, asked, "How is this possible?"

Grandma put her arm around her shoulder and said softly, "Stay with us, dear, you will understand shortly!"

Graybeard turned to Conor, saying, "Lad, you have made a wonderful decision to include them in our small band of confidants! I have felt that Janet should have been aware of us long before now!"

Graybeard then turned back to Grandpa. "I have things to attend to before the festival of the telling starts. So if you would like, you can take them by the village, and show them around; it's all but deserted now that everyone is headed for the clearing!" Then he added, "You know where you can be seated for the ceremony." With that he tipped his hat to the ladies and with a wave was off up the trail.

Grandpa said, "Follow me!"

They continued down the path in the direction Graybeard had gone, and after about fifty yards, they came to another path that led to the right, away from the main trail, and they followed it.

"This trail encircles the village, but the village is surrounded by sticker bushes and wild berries with no apparent openings or paths leading in."

But as grandpa stopped at a rocky area covered by bushes, he stepped on one rock and then another that released a rope and pulley system raising the sticker bushes just enough to allow them to enter. Once they get inside the barrier of bushes, they found another path.

"If you will just come this way, you can see most of the village from here," Grandpa instructed over his shoulder. The vegetation thinned out as they stopped at a grove of pine trees. There before them was what looked like a picture out of a child's storybook. There were hundreds of small, thatched-roofed houses on the ground. Some were built in the lower branches of the trees with rope walkways leading from one to the other. Most of the houses on the ground had small little gardens, with vegetables that grew close to the ground and didn't get very large, like okra and strawberries. The bigger plants, like corn, carrots, or melons were grown in the fields away from the village or provided by Grandpa and Grandma. The grounds around them and the houses were kept clear of any rocks, twigs, and pine needles. The five stared in wonder at the sight before them.

Grandma said, "It takes my breath away every time I see it!"

There were ropes hanging down with knots in them for climbing. Stairways were built into the side of tree trunks leading to the homes off the ground. Conor gazed in awe at elevators with ropes going to hand-cranked winches for hauling items up to the homes. Janet counted six water wells spaced throughout an irrigation system leading to all the gardens.

"Good heavens this is amazing!" said Janet.

"Amazing is definitely the word!" Conor replied

They continued on around the path with "Wow," "Look at that," and "Unbelievable" being the extent of the conversation.

When they reached the main trail again, Grandpa stopped and said, "When we get back to the house, I will show you how to inform them you are coming out here, so there are no surprises. Never walk through the village. Stay on the paths; we don't want anyone getting hurt!"

With that he said, "Let's go!" They followed him on down the walkway for another forty yards or so when again he stopped and motioned for them to leave the walkway. They walked behind some tall brush until they came upon two wooden benches, which had been built about four feet apart. Then Grandpa whispered, "You three need to sit here, facing the brush! Be as quiet as you can! It will all start in a few minutes!"

He and Grandma set on the other bench and waited.

Conor and the ladies sat there and soon began to hear voices coming from the other side of the brush. Some were talking, others laughing, and some just a low mummer. Slowly there were more and more voices, and they grew louder with each second that went by. The three of them were so exited they could hardly sit still. Through the brush they could see glimpses of bright colors, but nothing more.

Graybeard stood on a knoll to one side of the big clearing, watching the villagers enter and take their places. Some sat on little wooden benches that had been placed in a semicircle around the speaker's platform, and some preferred to sit on the naturally

formed seats of tree roots and rocks that encompassed the clearing. He smiled as he looked around the area.

Gary and the rest of the volunteers have done an exceptional job this year, he thought. Then he noted that two of the teachers had the children twelve years and under sitting in one section. They were ready to take them on a field trip to the stream after he made the introductions, and before the telling started. He took in a big breath, let it out, and then headed for the speaker's platform.

He noticed the thirteen and older children were seated in the front row. *Only nine!* he said to himself. Just before starting up the steps, he turned to look for Kasandra, the village healer. He spotted her over by the main entrance, just coming in. Looking around, she noticed him motioning her over to him. She waved back and started working her way through the crowd. She stopped along the way to adjust a bandage or two and to inquire if her remedies were working.

He was patiently waiting when she finally made it to him.

"Good morning, Father!" she said as she hugged his neck.

"Good morning, dear. How are *all* your patients doing? Well I hope!"

"Very well!" She smiled at him, knowing he was teasing her about how long it took her to reach him.

In a serious tone he said, "Have you taken notice that since the last telling three years ago, we have no news of babies on the way?"

"Yes, I have," she replied, "and I'm very troubled about it!"

They noticed things were about to start and took their seats on the platform.

As they sat down, Graybeard saw that most of the people had ceased their greetings to one another and were starting to settle down. He leaned over and quietly said, "We must talk of this more!"

"I agree!" she answered. "Come to my house tonight after the telling. I have fresh-baked oatmeal cookies!" Knowing how much

he loved her cookies, ever since her mother passed on, she had tried to have him come over as often as she could. She didn't like him living alone and worried that he was not eating right or taking good care of himself. But he insisted he was getting along just fine.

"Cookies! Ah, I will bring some fresh milk," he said with a big grin.

By now the people had all entered and found seats. Graybeard stood and moved to the center of the platform. As he walked over to the podium, he recalled his first telling, oh so long ago. Looking down at the bright faces of the young ones seated close to the platform, he saw the same expressions of excitement and wonder, which he had known those many years before.

He smiled and raised his hand to quiet the people.

"Welcome to the festival of the telling. Before we start, we have guests to introduce. We have five Big people with us today! I would like to start with the two you all know very well, our beloved friends Conor and Faye!"

Graybeard turned to the right with a sweep of his arm, and like magic the brush in front of them slid to the side. The crowd broke into applause as Grandpa and Grandma stood and waved to them all. Graybeard looked to the right of the stage and gave Gary and three other men who had pulled the ropes that parted the bushes a big thumbs up. When the applause died down he continued.

"As we all know, the Lord called home their son Conor the Fourth and his wife, Sara, last year. They will be dearly missed until we see them again in heaven. But tonight we are adding three more dear friends to our trusted circle! You have heard the elders and I speak of them many times! I am proud that all of you finally get to meet Janet Cook, her daughter Brittany and Conor O'Brian the Fifth!"

Graybeard turned to the left with a sweep of his arm, and the bushes shook but didn't move. He looked to the left and saw four

men straining on the ropes, but nothing was happening. There were a few chuckles and hoots from the crowd and then a loud pop as the rope broke and the four men landed on their rears.

The bushes started to fall over; Conor caught them and started side stepping them to the left with his head over the top, grinning. The whole place broke into a roar of laughter with some even falling off their seats, holding their sides.

Conor went back to Brittany's side, and the three of them were caught up in the contagious laughter. The grandparents and Graybeard, along with the crowd, burst into a five-minute belly roll! When everyone finally quieted down, the ice had been broken, and a warm feeling of friendship settled over all of them.

After wiping the tears of laughter from his face, Graybeard raised both arms and in a loud voice proclaimed, "Hear ye! Hear ye! Hear ye! I proclaim this to be the time of the telling to this the fifth generation in the new world."

An overwhelming *hooray* came from the crowd along with more applause. The two teachers with the youngest children lined them up, and they were soon off on their little field trip. Among the group was Angela, the teacher's daughter, and Ahnika, Kasandra's daughter.

The teenagers in the front were all now totally focused on Graybeard.

"You are the next generation!" He said as he spread his arms to indicate all the teenagers. Looking up and scanning the crowd for the faces of their parents, he continued, "It is time that you learn from where we came and who we are!"

The oldest of the children, Trey, thought to himself, *Who we are? I know who we are. We are kids, people. What's he mean, who we are?*

Trey looked up to hear Graybeard saying, "…are not normal size for most humans, you see, we are smaller, much smaller."

Now Conrad's hand shot up as if he was still in a classroom.

Graybeard was having a hard time holding back a smile as he addressed Conrad, "Yes, Conrad, what is it?"

"What do you mean we are smaller?"

"Well, Conrad, most of the people that live on this earth are five to six feet tall. Your dad, although he is tall for a Tiny, is only just over one foot tall."

After a second or two of thinking about it, there were a lot of oohs and ahhs from the children along with some puzzled looks.

"Let me explain!" continued Graybeard

"We are the, or rather, you are the fifth generation since we were brought to this country from England in 1919. Now I know you have studied some history in school."

Most of the children nodded their heads yes.

"You know that we live in the state of Tennessee, which is in the country of the United States of America. You also know about towns and cities. But what you do not know is that we are living here away from towns and cities for our protection! We must remain separated and away from the Bigs!"

This time it was Chais's hand that shot up. He was one of the boys known as the three musketeers. because they were all three born within a ten-day period of each other. And also the three of them were always seen running around together.

"Yes, mister Chais, what is it?"

"You said 'stay away from the Bigs!'"

"Yes!"

"A big what?" This brought laughter from the crowd.

"No, not a big, I mean...not...ahem... What I meant to say was to stay away from the big people. That's what I meant. We Tinys call them Bigs."

Another hand went up, this time it belonged to Brandyn.

"Yes, Brandyn?"

"Why do we have to stay away from the Bigs? Are they bad people? Would they hurt us?"

THE TELLING

"No!" Graybeard answered. "Most people are not bad, but some, just a few, mind you, are just very curious, and that is not good for us."

This time it was Dowen, another one of the three musketeers, who raised his hand and asked, "Why is being curious bad?"

"Well, it's hard to explain… All right, think of it this way. When you see a baby animal, you want to hold it, play with it, and keep it, right? Some of the Bigs think of us kind of like that. They don't think we are animals, but they would want to pick us up and play with us. And most likely want to keep us."

"Because we are small like some of their toys?" asked Dowen who had been taking this all in.

"That's right, like a toy," answered Graybeard, enjoying all this interaction with the kids.

"Are there any Bigs living near us?" asked Nathan, the younger brother of Conrad and the third musketeer.

"No, Nathan! They live very far from here. We are safe here, in the forest!"

Kariya, who was the youngest child at the telling, raised her hand.

"Yes, Kariya, what is your question?"

She stood up. When she did, the top of her head was barely even with the other children's heads that were still seated. "Have you ever been hurt by a Big?"

Graybeard smiled as he pulled on his beard and said, "No, I have not. My best friend is a Big." He pointed to Grandpa, Conor O'Brien III. "Yes, yes, I know I said that Bigs were bad for us, and it's true with a very few exceptions, and the O'Briens are a very special exception.

"Now you all know Grandpa and Grandma O' Brian, and you know they love you and would never hurt you. Well, their grandson, Conor, Miss Brittany and Miss Janet love you too, and they only want to help keep you safe. I know it's hard for you to understand that some people, big or small, can do bad things,

but that's a lesson you must learn. The world outside of our little village is full of people and things that can hurt you. But let me emphasize that most people of all sizes are good. The thing you need to remember is it's better for us if the world outside does not know of or ever find out we even exist. You see, it was the great, great, great grandfather of Mr. O'Brien that brought my great- great- great-grandparents here to live in America."

Half a dozen hands went up all at once.

"Wait, wait, now that you have heard of the Bigs, tomorrow at school your teacher will tell you all about our history and how we came to be here."

This time Venessa, the next to the oldest girl, raised her hand.
"Yes, Venessa?"
"Why can't you tell us now?"
"Well, I…"
"Please!" was the cry from all the children.
"Well I…suppose… If you really want to know!"

He was having a hard time holding back a grin. He loved to tease the young ones!

"Okay!" he said, and he burst out laughing and signaled the teacher to come up.

The teacher, the children call Mr. Vaughn, came up onto the platform toward Graybeard, smiled, and winked. Then, turning to face the children, he found them all sitting quietly, watching his every move and gesture. As he pulled up a stool that was nearby, he sat and readied himself for the stories he loved to tell the most. He too remembered how excited he was at his first telling. He began…

"The best way to explain our history is through the Telling. This has been told to each and every generation."

Graybeard walked up to him and handed the teacher a very large, leather-bound book.

"Before I start, let me explain this book!" He held it up so that all could see.

"It is very old, as you can tell, and the first records of our linage were written by John Ashley. This account you are about to hear has been handed down to each generation. John was Count Edward Hawk's right-hand man. This is the only written record of our forefathers and of us Tinys. Each generation adds its part. Vaughn opened the old book and very carefully turned to the first page.

"Our story begins with…"

First Records of the 1657 Rescue

The year is 1657. In England, the young Count Edward Hawks was worriedly pacing the floor. He had just summoned his two best men, Luke and John. He had known these men all his life. They had served his father before him and were like older brothers. Entering the Count's sitting room, a servant announced, "Sire, they are arriving and will be here in a moment."

"Very good, send them right in!" replied the Count excitedly.

The two men had been at the practice field training and testing their fighting skills. John and Luke had been waiting for the Count to send them on a special mission. Now he had called for them, and both were ready to do go anywhere for this man they loved as a brother.

The mood in the old castle was one of grief and despair. So many bad things had happened recently.

Edward's father, Count William, had fallen ill and died only a few months back, and it was only a year earlier that Edward's mother had passed quietly in her sleep. The sudden loss of his wife had taken its toll on Edward's father, William, and his health failed rapidly. Now Count Edward, at the age of eighteen,

was alone and in charge of a large estate in the north of England and several businesses his father had founded. Losing both his parents in such a short amount of time had hit Edward hard, but the duties of running what was now Hawks & Company helped by keeping him busy.

Now this! A mad man named Hobart and his band of cut-throats had captured some of the little ones, and no one knew where he had taken them. This man Hobart was a ruthless pirate who had fled France, a few years ago, to escape hanging. When Edward's father, Count William, discovered the Tinys, Hobart's men stumbled onto them at the same time. Count William, with his men and the help of the Tinys, had defeated Hobart and captured most of his men. Unfortunately Hobart and a few others had managed to get away. Now Hobart was back in England and taking his revenge.

Count Edward had sent men out to scour the country, looking for them. Finally after almost a month, he had news!

John and Luke quickly climbed the stairs to where the Count was waiting. As they came to the open door of the sitting room they hesitated, as it was not proper to enter without be acknowledged.

"Come in, my friends!" the Count told them, "I have news to share" He motioned for John to close the door as he put one finger to his lips. When the door had closed tightly, he came over and greeted them with a slap on the shoulder. "Come sit, we must not let anyone overhear our plans."

"You have good news, sire?" Luke inquired.

"Aye! That I have. Our spies have found out where he holds them, and we must be quick before he moves them again. He has brought them back to the ruins of that old castle he's been using as a base. It's only two days' ride, and once we are there, we will mount our attack and take them back!" announced the count.

John spoke up, "Sire, if we mount a full-scale attack, surely they will know we are coming and hide the little ones again." The

count's champion and lifetime friend, he was very loyal to the Hawk family. At five-foot-seven inches, he was average size, but he was stronger than he looked and very versed with the weapons of the day.

Count Edward stood and slowly paced back and forth, thinking. "Of course you are right, John, but what can we do that will not alert them?"

"We should take only a small band. That way we could hit them—" John started to say.

"No, wait!" Luke interrupted, "I believe the best way to get inside is for only two to go. John and I could sneak in. We could dress like Hobart's guards, bluff our way in, and fight our way out if we have to. They will not expect only the two of us." John's best friend and fellow orphan, Luke, was also the count's champion.

Count Edward and John both nodded their heads in agreement. "I do believe that could work!" agreed the count. "But what of me? Surely I must go!"

"No, sire! You would be in much danger. Should we be discovered, it would be very hard for us to protect you," John exclaimed. "You are better needed here, for if we should fail, then who will try again, if not you?"

"Aye! You are right again, my friends. It will not be easy, staying here while you two go off to fight my battles. But let it be done as you say."

"But what of Hobart? How did he take the little ones in the first place?" asked John.

"As you know, Hobart and my father clashed a long time ago when the Tinys still lived in the Dark Forest. Hobart and some of his men were driven off, and he swore he would come back. A few years ago he returned from France with what I'm sure is ill-gotten wealth and bought that old, run-down castle. He had not bothered any of the Tinys or us until he captured some of the Tiny men while they were on a quest. The Tinys wanted to go back to the Dark Forest where they once lived to retrieve some-

thing of value they had left there long ago in a cave. The little ones had decided it would be best to travel without an escort, thinking it would be easier for them to travel unseen. But Hobart had placed a spy in our village. That's how he knew of them and when they would be alone," answered the count.

"But why has he taken them?" asked John.

"Hobart is a man mad with power and wealth. I have been told that he believes the little ones have the knowledge of how to conjure up gold! The fool!" the count explained. "He is convinced they know how to turn lead into gold. He must be beating and torturing them, trying to get the secret of out them, a secret they never had!"

"Why don't they just tell him of the treasure that is here and save themselves from all that pain?" John asked.

"That, my friend, you will have to ask them yourself! They have always been very loyal to my father, and to me. I have pledged to protect them and have failed! You must bring them back!"

"Aye, that we will, sire, and as for Hobart, if I find him, I would have him at the end of my sword!" John said.

So the count sent them off with "Go now, and God's speed to you both!"

Two days later, John and Luke drove their wagon into the small village that sat next to the old castle where Hobart held the little ones. No one paid them much attention. They had managed to find two of Hobart's men patrolling outside of the village and had taken their uniforms. They fit well enough, and the villagers were used to seeing his men traveling back and forth. They had waited until nightfall to enter the village, and as they came closer to the back gate of the old, broken-down castle, they could see there were only two guards on duty. As they slowly approached the gate, one of the guards came to the center of the road, blocking their way. "Halt!" he commanded.

"Whoa!" John said to the team of horses as he brought them to a stop.

"What be your business here?" the guard demanded.

"Hobart's business, you darn fool. Who else would have us out in the middle of this damp night when we could be home sleeping next to our wives?" Luke said.

"And a nice fat one he has too!" said John, and they all laughed.

"Go on then, and get your work done so you can go home to that fat wife!" said the guard, and again they laughed.

Once past the gate, they swung the wagon around and parked it so as to have a straight run at the gate when they escaped. As they climbed down from the wagon, Luke said, "Hopefully fooling the cell guards will be as easy."

John looked over at him and saw he had a big grin on his face.

They did manage to get into the cellblock without encountering anyone. But at the cell that held the little ones, there were two very big guards. John walked right up to the one he assumed was in charge. "Hobart has instructed us to transport these creatures"—he pointed to the cell holding the little ones—"to a new location right away!" And he started for the cell.

The head guard held up his hand. "Let me see your orders!" he demanded.

"But of course," John said as he reached into his cloak and drew his knife and pointed it at the guard's throat.

"Will this do?" he asked jokingly.

Luke too had his knife out and pressed against the other guard's belly. With his free hand, he reached over and took the guards' swords and tossed them aside. John removed the cell keys from the first guard's belt, forced them into an empty cell, tied and gagged them, and locked them in. They opened the cell where the little ones were and told them they had come from Count Hawks. As they were putting them into the wagon, the guards for the next shift came around the corner. It was a dark night, so the guards did not see the Tinys being lifted into the wagon.

THE TELLING

"What's your business here?" one of the guards asked.

"Hobart's business. Who wants to know?" John demanded.

"I do, the captain of the guard," the captain announced.

John, trying to buy time so that Luke could get the little ones into the wagon, walked over to confront the two Hobart men. "Oh, good evening, Captain. I didn't recognize you in the dark."

Before the captain could see that John was not one of his men, John attacked, punching the captain on the chin and sending him falling backward to land on his back, out cold. John then jumped the remaining guard and wrestled him to the ground before the guard could draw his sword.

Meanwhile Luke picked up the last of the little ones and placed them inside the wagon.

John managed to hold the guard at bay until Luke could join him. John prayed that no one heard them fighting. Before the guard was able to call for help, Luke knocked him unconscious with the butt of this sword. The guards at the gate were inside a hut, trying to keep warm, and didn't hear the ruckus. John and Luke quickly climbed up on the wagon and headed for the gate. The same guard that stopped them when they entered came out to stop them again. He held up his lantern to see who it was. "And where be ye off to now?" he asked.

"You can bet it's not home to his fat wife on this cold night. That's for sure," John remarked.

The guard remembered them. "Ah, yes, the one with the fat wife!" Moving aside, he let them pass.

The guards were still laughing as the wagon disappeared into the night.

They had been traveling these dusty, tree-lined roads for two days. They had left the old wagon near a small village they had passed through and retrieved the coach they had hidden nearby. After leaving Hobart's castle, they had not headed straight back

to Corth Castle but instead had gone the other way in an effort to throw off any pursuers. Now the team of four fine horses were tiring, and it was taking all of his strength for Luke to maintain control of the coach and its precious cargo!

It has been a long, hard journey, John thought to himself as he sat looking out at the woods. He hoped that their success would please the count.

"Can you see it?" John asked form the back of the coach.

"Not yet, but it will be glorious to be home again," Luke said.

"But what of Hobart himself, the one who did this foul deed?" Luke questioned with a scowl on his face and fury in his eyes.

"If only we could have got at him, but we did not have enough time, mores the pity."

As the coach turned and started up the last of the winding roads that would take them through the hills to the castle they called home, John again turned his attention to the view alongside. It had been a hard and dangerous trip, and he longed to forget it. He was concerned that Hobart's men would soon be closing in on them and prayed that Luke and he would reach Corth before they did.

John's attention again returned to the view out of the coach. It was fast becoming fall, and the forest was ablaze with color. He always liked this time of the year, with the cool nights and clear, bright days. When he was a lad, he would walk for hours in the woods, just looking at the bountiful colors and listening to the leaves crunch under his footsteps. He loved the forest and that part of his youth. Back then there was always a new mystery just around the next tree or beyond the gully ahead. There were plenty of places to hide and play. Time to daydream of knights who fought from tall horses in shining armor. He loved to dream of gleaming swords, colorful banners, and decorated shields of old.

John's daydreaming was cut short when the coach hit a rut in the road, jarring him back to the present, just as Luke yelled, "Whoa!"

John quickly turned to see what it is that has caused Luke to give such an order.

Luke started yelling, "It's burning, it's burning! The castle is burning! What kind of trouble is this now?"

John, seeing the flames, ordered Luke, "Quickly now, turn off the road, and head into the woods over there!" as he pointed to the right where the trees were dense enough to hide the coach. He yelled to Luke, "Did you see?"

He asked only to find the answer in his friend's expression.

"Aye, that I did! Lord have mercy on us all, for what we have brought upon our Count."

Luke's head sunk to his chest as he asked, "How did they know to come here? We did not reveal ourselves to them. What kind of magic is this that they can find us so quickly?"

"It's not magic my friend, but the devil's work, I am thinking," John said as he moved to the front of the coach just in time to see the reins dropped, and the horses slowed to a stop.

"Come now, Luke!"

John shouted as he jumped out onto the ground.

"We must not let them find the little ones. I will drive, and you watch our backs to see if we are followed."

Climbing up onto the driver seat, John grabbed the reins and yelled, "Haw!" to the team of horses.

Looking back, he saw Luke standing up on the coach, facing the rear.

"I think I remember a gully not far from here."

"Aye! I remember; it's through there," Luke said as he pointed to his left.

"It should be large enough to hide the coach."

"Haw, now!" John shouted as he snapped the reins on the backs of the horses. "Haw, now!"

With a jump, they all pulled at once, sending the coach and its passengers deeper into the woods.

As the coach lunged forward, several tiny ohs, ouches, and even a few screams could be heard coming from the back of the coach.

"Sorry!" Luke yelled.

"We should have warned you. Is everyone all right?"

"Aye!" Came a reply from within the rear cargo area. "We are all right, you just caught us by surprise."

As they moved through the woods, Luke kept looking to their rear to ensure that they were not followed. Once again he called to those inside the coach.

"It will only be a little ways more, and then it will be safe to stop and let you out."

"Aye, thank you, sir. We could use a wee walk in the woods, if you catch my meaning!" replied the tiny voice from within.

After they had traveled four or five hundred yards into the woods, John finally turned the coach into a gully. Pulling back on the reins, "Whoa, whoa now!" he said as he pushed on the break lever with his foot to bring the coach to a halt As the coach stopped and the dust settled, John and Luke quickly looked around to make sure they were safe. John climbed up on top of the coach to get a better view.

"Do you see any sign of Hobart's men?" asked Luke.

"No, not a sign. I think we're safe enough here. Let's get them out! It must be very hard on them, being crammed in there for so long, besides being chased across the country by the likes of Hobart the Terrible and his evil bunch."

Luke entered the coach and lifted the rear floorboards to reveal a secret compartment, which had been added for the sole purpose of hiding and transport their tiny passengers.

Inside were twenty-four Tiny men. As they stood up, some were rubbing their eyes in an attempt to see better in the bright light of day.

John came around from the front of the coach and around to the rear, let down the tailgate, and one by one helped their passengers down to the ground.

After everyone was out of the coach, the oldest man looked up at John. "We owe you our lives and much gratitude, sirs. What can we say or do to repay you for saving us?"

"It is not us you need to thank, sir, but give your thanks to God. For it was only with His help and by His hand that our sire whose castle now burns, no doubt by the hand of Hobart, did we learn of you and your plight."

The old one lowered his head, closed his eyes and said nothing out loud. All the other Tiny people, who had been listening all along, stopped what they were doing and lowered their heads as well. After a few moments, the old one said aloud, "Amen" and raised his head; the others did the same.

The old one, seeing the look of surprise on John's face, said to him, "Do you suppose, sir, that because we are small and different from most, that we would not know and worship the Lord our God? I did as you suggested and gave thanks to the Lord for our deliverance and also for you, kind sirs, our deliverers."

John was somewhat taken aback and embarrassed. But then he replied, "Forgive me. I did not mean to imply such. I do though admit that up to now I did not think of you and yours as men and women, but more like children. My humble apologies."

The old man smiled at John. "You, sir, of all the Big people owe no apology."

"Thank you," said John. "May I inquire as to how this was done to you? How did all of you come to be so small?"

"We are as we have always been, small in stature and small in number. It has been so for as many generations as any can remember," the old one replied. "Do you think that we are safe here? Shouldn't we be moving on before they find us?"

Luke returned, having gone back the way they came to cover their trail.

"I hid our trail as best I could, but the coach wheels dug deep ruts I could not cover up, and I fear they will lead them to us."

Looking down at these precious little ones, John asked, "Is it true that you are all that is left of the ones that were caught?"

"Yes!" answered the old one. "We are all that remains. We started with thirty-six, but now only twenty-four are left after suffering under the hand of Hobart."

Luke reminded his friend, "John, it is growing near dusk, and we should be safe here until morn, don't you think?"

"Aye, I believe so! And these people need to rest and have a meal. Will you care for them while I go and see what has become of our homes and the Count?"

"I will, but you must take care not to be seen by Hobart or his men!" Luke said.

"Fear not, I will return before the night has passed!" John said as he unhitched the lead horse and climbed on. "If I do not return, you must see them to safety, my friend!"

Luke shook his friend's hand and said, "God willing we will both take care of them. Now go, and God be with you!"

John had spent about an hour going the long way around to come up behind the castle. It was not quite dark yet, and when he came closer, he saw that it was not the castle that was burning but the farmers burning off the fields after they had finished the harvest. John was very relieved that he and Luke had been wrong about the fire, but he was still very cautious as he approached the back gate of the place he called home. Knowing most of the guards, he called out before getting too close, "Hale the castle?"

The guard answered back, "Who say ye?"

"John Ashley."

The door on the gate flew open, and out came the guard. "John? Is it truly you? We thought the worst had become of you!"

"I am fine, my friend, and how is the Count?" John asked as he rode up to meet the guard whom he now recognized.

As the guard came up to the horse and took hold of the bridle, he said, "He is well and worried about you and Luke, and he has left orders for you to see him right away! What news have ye brought?"

John dismounted and started across the courtyard. He turned and with a wave said, "First, I must see my Count. Have someone tend to my horse."

"Yes, sir!" the guard replied and handed the reins to a servant standing nearby. "Here, see to his horse!"

Once inside, John found Count Edward sitting alone in his library. He rushed in with a happy shout. "Sire!"

"John!" he shouted out. "Thank the Lord you are safe!" Forgetting protocol, he got up and ran over to meet the friend he had known all his life. They clasped each other's arms. "I thought that you and Luke might be lost to me!" he said.

"And I feared for you and the castle when we saw the smoke and flames!" answered John.

"The castle smoke? What smoke?" Edward questioned as he led his friend over to sit next to his chair. Then he could see the light of knowledge come on in his face. "Oh! You saw the farmers burning the fields!"

"Aye, and we thought for sure that Hobart had burnt this place," John answered.

Edward looked at John with concern. "This man would do such a thing? Surly he would not dare to come against my men and me? Not after what my father did to him at the Dark Forest."

"That and more, my Count!" John exclaimed. "He is a terrible man. He treats his subjects with contempt and cruelty. He had mistreated the little ones so that scarcely twenty-four men are left!" John said.

"Only twenty-four you say? Why, when he stole them from here, they counted more than thirty-five! What did he do to them?" Count Edward asked.

John shook his head. "We have yet to learn the truth of his deeds.

Edward paced back and forth, thinking.

John, who was Edward's father's captain of the guard and had known Edward all his life, thought as he waited, *He has grown into a fine man that William would be proud of!*

Edward slumped in his chair, his head in his hands, and tears formed in his eyes. "I have failed them!"

"No! My friend, you have saved them twice. Once when your father and you brought them here to live and learn and become the God-fearing people that they are today, and now from the likes of this Hobart. But this mad man is very powerful, and he will not stop until he finds them again!" John reminded Edward.

"Yes, I know you are right. I have gathered all of the Tinys from their village in our nearby forest and had them brought here inside the castle. But If Hobart is as powerful as you say, these walls may not protect them. We must protect them at all costs. My father and I swore to protect them and keep them safe. Now we must do what I fear the most!"

"What is it you fear, my count?"

"I must ask a great deal of you, my friend." Edward said.

"Ask what you may, and I will give as I can," John replied.

"You must take the little ones far from here!"

"What? Take them away?" cried John. "But they are your friends! How can you protect them if they are far from you?"

"We must do this. They will not be safe if Hobart knows where they are," Edward said.

"Go get Luke and the little ones and bring them here for now. We will make plans as to where you must go to keep them away from Hobart and safe!"

John did as he was commanded and soon returned with the Tiny men and Luke.

While the Tiny men and their families were being reunited, Edward told Luke of his plan to have the Tinys taken far away from Corth Castle.

"Aye! I can see you are right, but how are we to do this, and where can we take them that would be safe?" asked Luke.

"Are you both willing to give up your home here and take on this task?" the Count asked.

"Aye! You know John and I have no family here. It was your father, God rest his soul, who took us in as orphan children and raised us as his own, so we leave little behind, save you, sire. We leave this castle we have called our home with heavy hearts, for I believe we can never return."

Edward stood and said, "It falls to you and John to take them and care for them. I have thought on it and believe you must go far from here, even as far as Ireland!"

"Ireland? That is wild country. How would we live there?"

"I can help; I have a great treasure, and as much as you need, you shall have!" exclaimed the Count.

"But, my Count, we only need a small ship that Luke and I can sail, and the supplies to see us through."

Count Edward Hawks looked long at his friends and smiled. He went over and pulled on the cord that hung nearby that summoned his servant. He turned to his friend and said, "You, sirs, are truly my champions and my friends! You shall have all you need!" A servant appeared in the doorway. Count Edward turned and said, "See to it John and Luke have all that they ask for, and send in the captain of the treasury!"

"Very good, sir!" replied the servant and quickly left to do his Count's bidding.

"The captain of the treasury?" John questioned. "My Count, we need only some food and a few supplies for the journey. We cannot take any of your fortune."

"Ah!" exclaimed the Count. "That's where you are mistaken, my faithful friend. You see, it is not my fortune; it belongs to them!"

"To the little ones? But how? I have seen this treasure, and it fills most of the catacombs beneath this very room," asked John. "How did they come by such a thing?"

The count smiled and motioned for his friend to sit down in one of the chairs, and then he continued, "As you recall, it was my father that first came upon them in the Black Forest these many years ago. They were trying to live in the forest, but because they feared the Big people, they stayed mostly in caves. My father stayed with them for some time and befriended them and asked them if they would come to live in his castle. He swore on his honor to protect and provide for them. At first they were reluctant, but after he took a few to see the castle, they agreed to come and live here. After they had grown to know him and the family as friends and providers, they told him of a treasure they had found in a sea cave. They took him to it and told him to take it back to the castle and to use it to help both his family and them. The count of this treasure was thirty-five chests of gold coins, two hundred chests of silver coins and bars, eight chests of diamonds and jewels. Most all of it remains here today, and you, sir, will have whatever they need of it."

"But we cannot travel with such a treasure; it is far too dangerous to do so!" John exclaimed.

"I will send it to you by ship as farm equipment as soon as you have settled," the Count explained. "Now go, and may God bless you and Luke and each who choose to protect these little ones! I will miss them as I would miss my own children!"

After bidding farewell to John and Luke and the Tinys, the little ship full of supplies and around four hundred little ones left on the long journey to Ireland.

Vaughn closed the book of the telling and looked down at the children sitting there, wondering what was next.

Trey was the first to speak, "What happened to them? Did they go to Ireland?"

And the others were all saying, "Tell us more; tell us more, please!"

"Well, we don't have any written records of what happened next. We can only speculate. But we assume that they did indeed go to Ireland and most of them stayed there for a long time. We do however have a record that tells us some of them must have returned to England, and later on in 1917 they got in real trouble! Do you want to hear that account?"

"Yes! Yes!" All they children said.

So the teacher opened up the telling book once more and began to read.

The Raid of 1917

The Big people village of Blyth where the Tinys were living was on the rugged northeast coast of England. It was a small out-of-the way place not well known or traveled, an ideal place where the little ones could live and work in harmony with the villagers. They had been there since the mid 1700s; some had chosen to live in the village but most in the caves nearby. These little ones were the descendants of those rescued from Hobart the Terrible back in 1657. It was rumored that another group was taken to Ireland, but no one knew for sure if that was just a tale or truth.

Then it happened. One of the village fishermen and his young nine-year-old son were out fishing like they had done so many times before. They had sailed out much further than usual because fishing was very poor close to shore, and they needed a good catch, for it had been weeks since they had caught anything.

A huge storm came up very suddenly and carried them far out to sea. The year was 1917, and England was at war with Germany. The storm blew them dangerously close to waters patrolled by the German Navy, and as luck would have it, a German gunboat saw them and stopped them for questioning. The Germans naturally assumed that the fisherman was there to spy on them. They beat him and tried to get him to confess he was a spy, but he was not. The German captain became very angry and told the man if he did not confess, they would beat the boy and throw him overboard. The fisherman became very afraid and wanted to save his son, so he told them the only secret he knew. He told them that in his village a great treasure of gold was hidden. They did not believe him at first, so they picked up his son and

started to throw him overboard, but the man cried out and told them to look under his son's shirt. They set the boy down on the deck and pulled his shirt off over his head. When they did, they found a strip of leather tied around the boys waist with a small pouch attached to it. One of the sailors pulled the pouch loose and opened it to find a single gold doubloon!

"*Gold*!" he exclaimed, holding it up for all to see. "Das is *gold*!"

The German captain saw this as a chance to become wealthy and decided he would raid the village and grab the plunder for himself; however, he told his crew that they were doing it for the fatherland. It was very dangerous to go near the coast of England, and the captain knew this. But the chance to find a great treasure was too much to resist. So, he ordered the prisoners to be locked up below.

"Take these two below, and put them in the irons!"

"Lieutenant Kruger, bring us about, and set a course for the coast of England!" the captain ordered.

"Yavole, my captain!" Kruger said as he nodded to the helmsman and then watched to make sure they were on the correct course. Seeing that they were now headed for the English coast, he told the captain, "On course, Captain!"

"Das is good!" replied the captain. "Maintain a sharp lookout for Englander ships. We do not want to get our Strudels shot off, now do we!" He laughed at his own joke and then started to leave the bridge. "I will be in my cabin. Notify me when land is sighted."

When the captain had left the bridge, one of the junior officers, a young man of nineteen, came over to Lieutenant Kruger. "Sir, we have standing orders *not* to go near the Englander coast!"

"Yavole Hendrix, I know what our orders say, but he is the captain."

Later as they approached the coast, Lieutenant Kruger ordered the captain to be notified and the prisoners to be brought up to the bridge. As they stepped through the hatch with the prisoner in front of the guard, the guard gave the man a shove, sending him sprawling onto the deck.

"That will be enough of that!" shouted Kruger.

The guard snapped to attention and, clicking his heals together, said, "Yavole!"

Lieutenant Kruger noticed that both the man and the boy had their hands bound in shackles. He pointed to the shackles and ordered the guard, "Remove those!"

The guard started to question the lieutenant, "But the captain—"

"Never mind that!" snapped Lieutenant Kruger. "I said remove them!"

The guard removed his knife from his belt and cut their bounds. Once that was done, the lieutenant ordered him off the bridge. "That will be all. You are dismissed!" The guard turned red in the face and without saying anything snapped to attention, saluted, and left the bridge.

The lieutenant took the boy by the arm and led him over to where he could see the coast out of the forward-facing windows. "Is that where you live?" asked Lieutenant Kruger in a soft voice. Seeing his village, the boy's expression was all Kruger needed to know.

"Yes, sir," answered the boy.

"Sub Lieutenant Hendrix!" Lieutenant Kruger said in a commanding way.

Hendrix snapped to attention. "Yes, sir," answered the sub lieutenant who was at his station on the other side of the bridge.

"Come here, I have an assignment for you," Commanded Lieutenant Kruger said.

Hendrix crossed to stand by the lieutenant Kruger who bent down and whispered something in his ear. The sub lieutenant looked at Lieutenant Kruger with a questioning expression then smiled and said, "Yes, sir, right away, sir!" He then took the two prisoners by their arms and led them off the bridge.

A knock on the door awoke the German captain. After rubbing the sleep from his eye, he said, "Yes, what is it?"

"Sir, Lieutenant Kruger wishes to report that we have arrived at the Englander village, as per your orders!"

"Very well, I'm on my way."

"Yes, sir!"

The captain dressed quickly and joined Lieutenant Kruger on the bridge and asked, "Any sightings of enemy vessels?"

"Nin, sir." Replies Lieutenant Kruger as he stepped down from the captain's chair, and stood aside.

"Have you seen any troops in the village?"

"Nin, sir, only a few civilians"

"Civilians? How can you be sure they are not soldiers merely dressed as villagers?"

"Captain? Sir, this is not a military installation, and we are deep in Englander waters. We should leave."

"Leave? Not until we find the treas… I mean destroy the enemy! Bring the guns to bare!" ordered the captain.

"No! Captain, you can't do this!"

But the captain ignored the lieutenant's pleas and ordered, "*Fire!*"

The grass, mud, and stick huts were no match for the heavy guns of the German ship; the villagers never had a chance!

Elizabeth O'Rourke had been in the village only a few days. She had traveled from Ireland only a week ago and was on a mission to try to locate the lost group of little people that were thought to be in that part of England. She was the only Big person that

knew about the little ones in Ireland, or more clearly, the only one who had contact with them and knew where they were. Her father had taken care of them until his passing. She has been looking after them for five years now. So when they told her that they had lost contact with the group in England and wanted to try to find them, she volunteered to go.

When she had arrived at the village of Blyth, she told them she was looking for an uncle who was her last remaining relative. Earlier that day, while she was visiting one of the homes, she was just looking around the house, as her host was busy making tea, when she saw a rug had been crumpled up where someone had bumped it when they walked over it.

She bent down to straighten it, and in doing so she noticed there was a trap door under it. She quickly straightened it and acted as if she had not seen anything.

A trap door? she said to herself. Could this be the clue she was looking for?

Just then the German shelling began. The lady of the house ran out to see what was happening and was hit right away. Elizabeth was looking out the open front door when she saw the woman fall. Just then the windows blew in, and she fell to the floor and crawled over to where she had seen the trap door. She opened the trap door and dropped into a dark tunnel. Being more afraid than she had ever been before, she did the only thing she could think of and crawled as fast as she could in the only direction the tunnel led, hoping she was moving away from the attack and toward the hills.

She had crawled about one hundred feet in total darkness, scraping her knees as she went, when she thankfully saw a dim light ahead. Overhead she could hear and feel the exploding shells as the house she had been in only moments ago collapsed. She fell on her face and covered her head with her arms, fearing the tunnel would collapse. But it did not, and she just lay there for a while, sobbing. Then she thought she heard a voice, a

tiny voice coming from up ahead in the tunnel. There it is again, closer this time. "Are you all right?" said the wee voice as the tiniest of hands touched her arm. She raised her head to see one of the little people standing there.

"Thank God I found you!" was all she said, and she fainted!

After the shelling stopped, the captain ordered Lieutenant Kruger to form a shore party and search the village for the treasure. Kruger and his men tried to search through the wreckage of the destroyed and burning huts, but the damage was too much, and the fires still too hot. Lieutenant Kruger had ordered his men to spread out and find whatever they could.

He was alone when he came around the last remains of what had been the village meetinghouse. He noticed, through the smoke, what looked like two children standing next to an injured man. When he had passed through the smoke and came nearer, he saw that what he had thought were children looked more like miniature men. Not children at all! Just as the two little men saw him, and he yelled at them to halt. The smoke blew around him again, and he lost sight of them. By the time the smoke dissipated, they were gone.

Just then he heard his ship's horn sounding the recall, turning back toward the shore, he saw the reason for the recall. A British ship was approaching at full speed. It was a cruiser, a much larger ship than the Germans', and the cruiser's guns could shoot more than a mile further that the German guns could.

As he ran back to the shore boat where his men were clamoring aboard, he shouted for them to shove off. Back on board his ship, he was met by the captain,

"Well, did you find the treasure?"

"No, but I saw something amazing!" explained Kruger.

"I don't care about what you saw unless it's the gold!" shouted the captain.

"Did you look everywhere?"

Unable to contain his anger at the captain for being so stupid as to destroy the village before they had a chance to look for the treasure, Lieutenant Kruger answered, "No! You destroyed everything! We couldn't even get near most of the huts because of the damage and fires!"

"Nothing? You found nothing?" exclaimed the captain, choosing to ignore his first officer's anger. "Nothing! I risked my career, and you found *nothing*! Get out of my sight!"

Lieutenant Kruger left the bridge and went to his cabin.

Meanwhile, the Germans pulled up the anchor and started running from the British cruiser.

Now, below deck and in his cabin, Lieutenant Kruger was still furious with the captain. "I tried to tell that stupid man what I saw!" he said to himself. "Now I will fix him. I'll record everything that has happened in my journal, and when we get back to port, I will report what he did!" Kruger sat down at his writing table, opened up his journal, and started writing.

Back on the bridge, "Where are that fisherman and the boy? Bring them to me!" shouted the captain just as the first shells from the British cruiser exploded just off the bow.

"Return fire!" ordered the captain.

"No!" exclaimed Sub Lieutenant Hendrix. "Sir, they just want us to heave to. If you fire, they will destroy us!"

"We can out run them!" the captain said, and he again ordered, "Full speed, man the guns and prepare to open fire! *Fire*!"

Just then the sailor that was told to go get the fisherman and boy returned. "Captain, the prisoners are gone!"

"*Gone*!" shouted the captain. "How could they get away? Where did they go?"

But before the sailor could answer, the British ship fired a broadside of all its guns that found its target with deadly results.

The British guns proved to be more accurate and strike the smaller German ship, destroying everyone on board.

Meanwhile back in the tunnel, Elizabeth woke to find the little man trying to revive her.

He begged, "Please, it is only a few more feet, you must crawl, and then you will be in the cave where you can stand up."

Getting to her knees, she continued to crawl into the cave and found it lit by only three candles. As she slowly stood up and looked around, she saw another little man. This one was older, standing off to one side. The younger man was talking to the older one, quietly, so that she could not hear.

"She said, 'I have found you,' and she was not surprised to see me."

The old one looked up at her and said, "You are not of this village!"

Elizabeth sat down on the floor of the cave so that she could see them better and replied, "No, I am from Ireland, and I have been sent here by the Tinys who live there."

"I have no knowledge of anyone living in Ireland," the old one said, trying to trick her and find out who she really was and her real reason for being in the village, for he had learned that she was looking for a lost uncle. She smiled and reached down her blouse and retrieved a small, leather pouch. She set it down on the floor and opened it.

"I do not lie, nor do I fault you for your suspicions, so see for yourself the proof of what I say," she said as she pointed to the open pouch.

The young one started to move as to go over to the pouch, but the old one stopped him. "Wait, I must see this proof myself!"

He walked over and looked inside to find it contained a ring. "A ring belonging to a Big person is no proof of what you say!" he announced.

Elizabeth slowly reached inside the pouch and removed the ring. As she turned it around so that the old one could see the

crest inlayed in the red stone, she saw the old man smile from ear to ear!

"It sounds like the British troops have arrived!" said Elizabeth.

"Yes!" answered the young Tiny. "We must not be found here!"

"Is there a back way out of here?" asked Elizabeth.

"There is that, but I'm afraid the opening is too small for the likes of you, my friend!" said the old man.

"Then you two go quickly. I will be fine! I will *not* give you away to them or anyone else!" Elizabeth said.

Just then, someone yelled, "You there in the cave, come out, or I'll toss in a blooming grenade, I will!"

"Oh! Please don't! I'm English!" Elizabeth exclaimed.

She then turned to the two Tiny ones and said, "Go now! I will come back as soon as I can."

"God keep you, miss!" the old man said, and out of sight they went.

She turned back to the tunnel entrance and yelled, "I'm coming out; don't shoot!"

Lieutenant Hobart yelled at the sergeant, "Throw it! I ordered you to throw it!"

"Sir, I can't, there's a lady in there!" answered the sergeant.

Now Hobart was waving the pistol all around and getting red in the face as he commanded, "That's an order, Sergeant!"

"Yes, sir, but that's a civilian in there, sir!"

Right in the middle of all this, Lieutenant O'Brien and the rest of the marines walked up. "What is going on here?"

Hobart turned around and said, "This man refuses to obey a direct order. Arrest him!"

Lieutenant O'Brien looked over at the marine sergeant. "What's this all about, Sergeant?"

"Sir, the lieutenant here ordered me to throw a grenade into that cave, and I believe there is a civilian woman in there!"

O'Brien turned back to Hobart, "Is that true? Is there a woman in there?"

Hobart was outraged at being questioned and replied, "I gave a direct order, and he"—he pointed to the sergeant—"refused to obey it!"

While this had been going on, Elizabeth had managed to crawl back out of the tunnel and was standing beside one of the marines, "May I say something?" she calmly said.

Lieutenant O'Brien turned to see, although a bit ruffled and dirty, one of the most beautiful, red-headed women he had ever laid eyes on! "Yes, ma'am!" was all he could say.

She continued, "My name is Elizabeth O'Rourke. I am here visiting, and they…I was…"

While she was talking, she looked around at the destroyed village and the home where she was, only moments ago, having tea! Seeing the massive devastation, she stopped speaking, broke down, and cried out, "Heavenly Father, what have they done?" as tears rolled down her face.

Then you could see the anger build up inside her as she turned and pointed to Lieutenant Hobart. "This man wanted a grenade thrown in that cave without finding out who or what was in there!" She pointed to the cave she had just exited. Then she came over to stand face to face with Hobart. "You! You would have killed me if the sergeant here had not questioned your order to throw a grenade in on *me*!"

Lieutenant O'Brien turned to Hobart. "Harry, what in the world were you thinking?"

"I don't have to answer that!" said Hobart.

O'Brien, seeing something was very wrong with his onetime friend, said, "Lieutenant Hobart, you are relieved of duty and will stand down. I'm placing you on report!" Turning to the marine sergeant, he said, "Sergeant, you will witness my orders!"

"Yes, sir!" said the sergeant.

Lieutenant O'Brien, seeing that all the men had gathered around, said, "All right, men, the village is secure, and we have

found only this one survivor! Sergeant, form a burial detail and tend to these poor souls!"

"Yes, sir! Right away, sir," the sergeant replied, and he turned to the marines. "Fall in!"

The men all snapped to, and then the sergeant assigned them to details. "Corporal, take six men and get these people buried proper like!"

"Yes, sergeant!" and off they went.

"Murphy and James, stand guard on the beach! Tom, you and Smith watch this side of the village and the road!"

"Yes, sergeant!" was all anyone said.

After the men had moved out and only Elizabeth, the sergeant, and the two lieutenants were left, Lieutenant Hobart started in again. "I gave an order, and he refused to obey!" he said, still waving the pistol around. The sergeant, who was standing closest to Hobart, waited for the right moment and then simply reached up and disarmed him.

"I'll take that, sir, if you don't mind," the sergeant announced as he tucked the pistol in his belt. Turning to address Lieutenant O'Brien, he inquired, "Would there be anything else, sir?"

O'Brien, trying desperately to hold back a laugh, shook his head and told the sergeant, "No, thank you, Sergeant, carry on!"

"Sir!" said the Sergeant as he saluted, turned, and walked off swiftly.

Lieutenant O'Brien remarked, "Harry and you too, Miss O'Rourke, we had better go down to the beach and wait for our ship."

Harry Hobart was still standing there with his mouth open and holding his hand like he still held the gun.

O'Brien took hold of Hobart's arm and, leading him, started off. He turned back to see Elizabeth still standing there. "You too, Miss! I believe you had best come along with us until we can figure out what to do with you. As you can see, there is nothing you can do to help here."

Elizabeth ran to catch up. Walking along side of him, she said, "I guess you are right, Lieutenant. I can return later for my things, if I can even find them." All the while thinking to herself, *What in the world am I to do now? I can't just leave the little ones here all alone to deal with this awful mess...* She stopped abruptly as if she has forgotten something. Lieutenant O'Brien stopped and turned around to see what was wrong.

"What is it, Miss?" he asked.

"I need to go back and find my bag! It has all my money and things! Can you help me try to find it?"

"Yes, ma'am!" He looked around for the sergeant, and seeing him on the beach, he called him over. "Sergeant!"

The sergeant snapped around, "Sir?" Seeing the lieutenant waving for him to come, he took off on the run. When he reached the lieutenant, he snapped to attention and saluted.

Lieutenant O'Brien returned the salute and said, "Sergeant, I need you to take over here while I return to the village to help Miss O'Rourke find some of her things."

"Yes, sir!"

"And have the corporal stay with the lieutenant." He pointed to Lieutenant Hobart who just stood there, staring out to sea. "Signal me when the ship comes back," ordered Lieutenant O'Brien.

As they walked back to the destroyed home where she was staying, the lieutenant asked, "What brings you to England, Miss O'Rourke?"

She was deep in thought, worrying what to do about the little ones. "Oh! I came here looking for some long lost friends," she said, not wanting to lie to him. "And you may call me Elizabeth, Lieutenant." She smiled.

He smiled back at her. "Well then, you must stop calling me Lieutenant, Conor O'Brien at your service! Now, what is it we are looking for?" he asked as they arrived at the remains of the home.

She started looking around in the rubble and picked up a few items of clothing and personal things like a comb and brush. She found her coat but on close examination saw that it had a hole in it.

Trying to lighten up the mood, Conor, seeing the coat said, "Boy! It's a good thing you were not wearing that!"

She laughed and tossed it back on the rubble pile. Then she thought of a way she could talk to the little ones without the lieutenant knowing. "Lieutenant, ah…I mean Conor, I can't find my purse, would you be a dear and watch that the remains of this house does not fall in and block me in while I go back in there and search for my purse?"

"I'll go, and you stay here!" he said.

"Thank you, Lieutenant, but I know where I sat, and I think you are a bit too big to get through the opening to the cave."

"Well *okay*, but here, take my lantern! And be quick about it!" he said with a big grin.

"Why thank you, Conor!" she returned to addressing him by his name. "I won't be but a moment," she said as she jumped down and crawled into the tunnel. Inside, she did not find the little ones as she had hoped, and she sat down to think what to do.

"Are you all right in there?" called Conor.

"Yes! I'm still looking for it," she answered.

"And what is it you are looking for, Miss?" a small voice asked.

She turned to see the young man that found her in the tunnel smiling up at her.

"Oh! Thank God! I was so worried that I would not see you before I had to leave."

"Leave?" questioned the little man.

"Yes, the navy officer is insisting that I should be taken back to port with them, and I can't refuse to go, or they might wonder why I would want to stay with no one left alive here. You do understand, don't you?"

"Why, yes, of course! And you must not worry about us, we have all we need right here in these caves."

From outside, "What's taking so long, Elizabeth? We need to get back to the beach!" Conor shouted.

"I think I found it; just one more quick look around and I'll be out!" she called back. Then to the little man she said, "I will be back with supplies and the means to get you out of here and to Ireland just as soon as I possibly can."

"Godspeed, Elizabeth O'Rourke! We will await your return." He then turned and was gone.

Love and Betrayal

When the British warship returned and sent a long boat to retrieve the shore party, Lieutenant O'Brien ordered all the men to board the boat, and as they all climbed aboard, he turned to Elizabeth. "I believe you should come along with us, Miss O'Rourke."

"I can't go. I must stay and…"—she looked back at the still burning village. "And help!" she said weakly, not really believing any of the villagers were in need of help anymore.

Standing next to the shore boat, O'Brien reached out his hand to her. "Come along now. There's nothing to do here."

Turning, she took his hand, and they boarded the boat.

When they get out to the cruiser and had boarded, O'Brien asked Hobart to take Elizabeth to the mess hall while he reported to the captain. Hobart, who had been quiet for some time, started another of his rants, "Oh! I see, send me off on an errand so you can fill the captain's ear full of nonsense about me. Well, you're not getting away with it! I'm going up to report that marine who refused my order, straight away!"

O'Brien looked around to see if anyone had seen or heard Hobart's comments, and determined the passageway was clear except for the three of them. He grabbed Hobart by the front of his coat, lifted him up, and slammed him against the bulkhead. *Bam*! "Look here, you sorry, spoiled, brat of a man! If you try

that, I will beat you to a pulp! Now take our guest to the mess as I said!"

As he released his hold on his coat, Hobart's head and shoulders slumped down as he slowly turned and started down the passageway. Elizabeth gave O'Brien a questioning look. "Go with him; it will be all right," he assured her.

She reluctantly started after Hobart and after a few feet turned around and looked back with the same questioning look. O'Brien, who was still standing there watching them, saw her look and shooed her with a wave. "Go on, go on!" he coaxed with a smile.

Once on the bridge, Lieutenant O'Brien reported to the captain all that they had found in the village. He also explained he had to place Lieutenant Hobart on report and why.

"Where is Lieutenant Hobart now?" asked the captain.

"I had him escort Miss O'Rourke to the mess," answered O'Brien.

"Miss O'Rourke?" questioned the captain, and then he remembered that O'Brien had reported bringing her on board. "Very good, Lieutenant. Well done! Now to other matters; did you find anything in the village that might give us a clue as to what in the blazes the Germans were interested in?"

"No, sir!"

"What about this…what's her name? Does she know anything?"

"Elizabeth O'Rourke, sir. I don't believe so. She said she was just visiting from Ireland, sir."

"Ireland is it? Hmmm!" the captain repeated and started rubbing his chin.

"Sir?" the Lieutenant asked.

"Yes?"

"Was there anything in the German logs that might explain their attack?"

"What? Oh, nothing, nothing at all! That will be all for now, Lieutenant," ordered the captain.

"Very good, sir!"

"Oh! And see to it that you question this O'Rourke woman a bit more on the subject. And send up Lieutenant Hobart."

"Aye, sir!" And the Lieutenant was off the bridge and headed for the mess hall.

While all this had gone on, Lieutenant Hobart and Elizabeth had arrived in the mess. As they sat down, a young orderly came over and asked them what they would like to have from the kitchen. Hobart, still in a funk, just waved him off, but Elizabeth stopped him with a request. "I wonder if I might have a cup of tea, if it's not a bother."

The orderly smiled. "Right away, Miss, and it's no bother at all!" He tipped his hat, and off he went.

Hobart, ignoring all that, was still stewing. "I'll fix him! My senior my foot!" he said under his breath.

The orderly arrived at the table with a pot of tea and some biscuits. Elizabeth thanked him with a smile, and, not wanting to set off another rant, simply asked Hobart, "Would you like some tea, Lieutenant?"

"*Tea*! Can't you see what O'Brien is doing? He is trying to ruin me! That dirty little…"

"Dirty little what?" asked Lieutenant O'Brien as he walked up to the table.

"What?" was all Hobart could get out.

Lieutenant O'Brien looked at Elizabeth, smiled, and pointed at a chair. "May I join you?"

"Please do," she said as she returned his smile.

Hobart started to say something but before he could O'Brien said, "Oh! The captain wants to see you *now*!"

After Hobart left, the lieutenant saw the orderly across the room and held up Hobart's tea cup and pointed to it. The orderly nodded in acknowledgement and brought him a fresh cup. Elizabeth took the pot and poured him a cup of tea.

"Biscuit?" she asked and offered him the plate.

"Thanks, but no," he said as he turned to look in the direction Hobart had gone. "What was he going on about this time?"

"He kept saying he would get even with you, and I believe he is the kind that will try to! I don't think he is in his right mind. Is he always like that? I mean I thought you called him friend back there in the village, didn't you?"

Conor shook his head and said, "I thought at one time we were friends, but after training and being assigned together, things changed."

"How do you mean?" she asked.

"Well, you see, I received my commission one month before he did," he said.

"One month? That's all!" Elizabeth exclaimed. "I'm afraid I don't understand."

"You see, in the navy, time of commission makes a big difference in who is put in command of jobs that are assigned. An officer that was commissioned even a day ahead of another out ranks him. And because I was commissioned before Hobart, he is obliged to follow my orders, not the other way around, as he would like it. It all has to do with ego, his I mean. That and the fact that once on board he found out that I was from the US, and he hates Yanks!"

Elizabeth just sat there with a funny look on her face. "You mean to say all that stuff that went on in the village was just to spite you?"

"Yes 'em! I mean yes ma'am, I'm afraid so!" He laughed.

"You will have to excuse my American slang. Sometimes it just slips out!"

She laughed and said, "I like the way you Yanks talk.!"

"Why thank ya, ma'am!" he said with his best southern drawl. They both laughed at that.

An orderly came up and said, "Your cabin is ready, Miss."

"Which one is it?" asked O'Brien.

"The executive officers quarters, sir," the orderly answered. "Will that be all, sir?"

"Yes, thank you," answered the Lieutenant. Then he said to Elizabeth, "I will show you to your quarters. But first, if you are not too tired, I need to ask you a few questions."

"Questions? What about?"

"The village, and the attack mostly. Do you mind?" he asked.

"No, not at all!"

"Okay then, let's start with why you were there. I remember you saying you were visiting. Is that correct?" he asked.

"Yes, I had been there for only two days." Staying with her story of looking for her uncle, she said, "I was trying to find my uncle who I thought was living in that village."

"I see; did you find him?" he asked.

"I'm afraid not. It seems he had moved on, and I'm not sure where," she answered.

Continuing, he asked, "How did you manage to get into that tunnel?"

She told him about the house and the woman preparing tea and seeing the trap door, and then she remembered the attack and started crying. "It was so brutal and senseless!" she exclaimed as she sobbed.

"Here now!" he said as he took out his handkerchief and handed it to her.

"I am sorry that we must go over this right now. It is important that you recall as much as possible while it's still fresh in your memory."

Still sobbing, "I know, it's just so sad!" she said as she dabbed her eyes.

"Do you have any idea what the Germans were doing there or what they were looking for?" he asked.

"I'm afraid not," She answered.

Then he asked her, "Do you understand German?"

"Yes, I do, I studied it in school," she answered.

"Did you overhear anything that might be helpful for us to understand what their mission was?" he asked.

She had stopped sobbing and looked at him for a moment, trying to figure out what sort of man he was. She needed help getting back to the Tinys. Would he help her? How could she ask him to help? After all, they just met. Although, she had liked him since she first saw him. Was he to be trusted with such a secret? And most of all, what would be his reaction if she told him? She decided to give him a little information to see how he would react.

"I heard the one called Lieutenant Kruger, I believe it was, telling the men to keep looking for something."

"Did he say what it was they were searching for?" O'Brien asked.

"I could not make out just what it was because of all the crashing and burning of the house."

"Do you have any idea what it might have been?" he questioned.

Just then a seaman came up to the lieutenant, saluted, and handed him a piece of paper. The lieutenant returned the salute and took the note.

"You'll excuse me please," he told Elizabeth as he turned away and scanned the message.

It read: "Have you deduced any useful information in your talks with the lady?" and it was signed by the captain.

Lieutenant O'Brien took out his pencil and wrote, "None so far," and handed it back to the seaman. "Return this to the captain," he ordered.

"Very good, sir!" the seaman replied. He wheeled around and was off down the passageway.

The lieutenant just sat there thinking for a minute, and then, noticing how tired she looked, decided to take her to her quarters so that she could rest up a bit. He smiled and said, "I believe we have been at this long enough. Let's get you to your room so you can freshen up and rest before the evening meal."

He stood and held out his hand. She smiled and took it, and he gently pulled her to her feet and led her to the room.

As they walked, he was thinking over their conversation and had a feeling that she knew something that she was not revealing. He had already dismissed the idea that she might be a spy back in the village when he saw her reaction to the destruction and deaths. He was confused and conflicted between trying to find out what the enemy was up to and his wanting to get to know her better. He had been attracted to her right from the first, and the attraction was growing with each minute he spent with her, but something in her manor or her eyes told him she was in trouble and needed help.

As they reached the door to her room, he took notice that they were still holding hands. He liked holding her hand, very much so. He opened the door for her, and as she started to enter, he asked, "If it's all right with you, I will be by to take you to the evening meal?"

She stepped just inside the room, turned around, and smiled. "Thank you. I would like that."

The evening meal was quiet with little conversation. Lieutenant Hobart was not around. Evidently he had been assigned some grungy job as punishment for his actions in the fishing village. He was not missed! Elizabeth and Conor just sort of sat there, looking at each other with silly grins on their faces. A lot was said, but few words were spoken.

Then Conor kind of snapped out of it and remembered something.

"I almost forget—I have one of the German officer's journal. You did say you could speak German?"

"Yes, I can," she replied.

"Can you read it as well?" he inquired.

"Yes, I can read and write German. Why?" she questioned.

"I was just thinking, if you don't mind, we could, or rather you could, read what's in the journal. So maybe we can find out just what they were after. That is if you're up for it?"

"Why, yes, I can do that. When do you want me to start?" she asked.

"Right now, if that's all right?" he questioned. "I just need to run down to my quarters and get the journal."

"Fine, I'll wait right here," she answered.

When he entered the room, Hobart was there, looking very upset. "So, you had to go and put me on report, did you!" he said angrily.

O'Brien, trying to make light of the thing, said, "Look, you are the one that went a little coo coo today in front of the men. I had no choice in the matter, and you know it!"

With that he went over, picked up the journal, and walked out.

Hobart was steaming and thought out loud, "I'll get even with him, so help me!"

A few minutes later, he headed to the dining room, ready for supper. Conor returned to the table where Elizabeth was waiting, and as he sat down, he handed her the journal. "Here it is!"

She opened it, and started to read. At first it only contained what would be normal day-to-day entries. Then right at the end, in the last page she found:

> March 12th, 1917
>
> We had come out of a very strong storm and were patrolling just off the Dutch coast when we came upon a small fishing boat. An Englander and his nine-year-old son were onboard. The captain, assuming that they were using the guise of fishing to spy on our ship movement, ordered the fishing boat brought alongside. The two Englanders were brought onboard for questioning. Sub Lieutenant Hendrix, who speaks English, was the interpreter. The Englander claimed to be just a fisherman, and they had been blown off course by the storm. But the captain would

not believe him and had him bound and beaten. But the man would not confess to spying, and after searching their boat, I found no evidence or spying equipment. Then the captain became very angry. He had one of our men pick up the young boy and threaten to throw him overboard. The Englander pleaded for his son's life. When they tied the boy's hands and feet, the man broke down, crying, saying that he was not a spy but that he would tell the captain a secret if he would save his son. He said that there was a large treasure hidden in his village. The captain did not believe him, so he had the men pick up the boy and hold him over the side of the ship. The Englander fell to his knees and begged the captain to look in the small pouch that was tied around the boy's waist. When they opened it, inside they found a gold coin. It was a very old coin, and that got the captain's attention. Then the captain disobeyed our standing orders not to go near the Englander coast, and he ordered us to go to the village of the fisherman.

When we arrived at the village, the captain ordered us to fire and had it destroyed even though I told him we could see no signs of a military outpost there, and all we saw were civilians.

Then he sent us ashore to search, not for the enemy or to see if there were any survivors, but to look for this so-called treasure! But the damage was too great, and because of all the fires, we could not do a good search. But while looking around, I saw something amazing! I saw two men that appeared to be only as tall as my boot! But when I tried to tell the captain, he of course had heard all the old stories of leprechauns, fairies, and the like and did not believe me and was only interested in the treasure…

Elizabeth gasped.

The Journal

Lieutenant Hobart was just about to enter the ship's mess hall when he overheard Elizabeth reading from the captured journal. He stopped just out of sight and listened. When he heard Elizabeth gasp aloud, he chanced a quick peek around the door and saw her drop the book and start to cry! Conor, not knowing what was wrong, was trying to console her. "What is it, Elizabeth? What's wrong?" he asked.

She turned and buried her head in his shoulder and wept. "I have betrayed them!"

"Betrayed who, the Germans?" he questioned.

She sat back in shock and pounded on his chest. "No, no, no!" Then she sank back against him, and as he put his arm around her, she softly said, "The little ones!"

Conor still did not understand what she is so upset about. "Don't tell me you believe in those fairy tales about little people and leprechauns and the like?"

She raised her head and looked around to make sure no one else was nearby, but she did not see Hobart hiding in the passageway. She looked Conor in the eyes and said, "I must help them. I believe you can be trusted, Conor! Lord, help me if I'm wrong!"

Now he was really confused. "What are you talking about?"

She went on, "I need your help, and I don't know where to start!"

"Is this about the attack?" he asked.

"No! Well, yes, in a way the attack has caused the problem; it's the German journal!" she picked up the book. "This thing must be destroyed!"

"What?" he said. "What is it that is in this book that makes it so important it must be destroyed? I didn't hear you read anything that would be a military secret."

She hesitated, and then continued, "It has nothing to do with military secrets! It's the story the fisherman told the captain. You see, I know it's true!"

"What?" he asked, "Are you telling me there really is a treasure in that fishing village and *that's* what the Germans were after?"

"*Yes*!"

Hobart heard someone coming down the passageway, so he headed back to his room. Once inside, he started his plotting. He thought himself, *That's it! I'll get even with him but good! I'll go back there, find that treasure, and I'll be richer than even my father, and with it I'll destroy Conor's life!* He laughed aloud.

Back in the dining room, Elizabeth was saying, "We can't talk here. Let's go to my room."

"*Okay*!" Conor said with a puzzled look on his face. They got up from the table and headed for the executive officer's quarters. Once they get there, Conor stopped at the door and said, "I'm not sure I should enter your room."

Elizabeth touched his arm and pleaded, "Please, I can't chance anyone overhearing what I'm about to tell you! Trust me, I can explain everything!"

Inside, Elizabeth sat on the bed, and she indicated to Conor to sit in the desk chair.

"I must tell you that I am having a very hard time believing this story of treasure. It's a bit much to swallow!" Conor started out.

"I know it is, Conor, but you must believe me when I tell you this is what I heard the Germans talking about!"

"*Okay*! I know that's what you said you heard, and I believe you. However, I find it very hard to believe a German officer would risk so much based on a fisherman's tall tale," he noted.

Elizabeth knew that somehow she must convince this man, whom she had grown to like very much, that she was telling the truth. But how could she tell the secret and yet protect the little ones?

She took a long look at Conor, and in him she saw goodness and caring, and she wanted to trust him; she needed to trust him. So, she asked, "Can I trust you to help me, Conor O'Brien?"

"Trust me? Of course you can trust me. But that's not the question. The question is can I trust you? I still don't know what you were really doing in the village and why you alone survived. Elizabeth, there is going to be an investigation by the Naval Command, and I need to have answers for them!"

She jumped up. "Investigation? Why? What are you talking about?"

He went over to her and took her hand. "Don't you realize that you are under suspicion?"

"*What*? Suspicion of what?" she asked, and she started pacing around the room.

"Please believe me. I don't think for a moment you had anything to do with what the Germans did. But the captain wanted me to find out why you were there and how you came to survive when everyone else was killed."

She sat back down on the bed and started sobbing.

"But I told you I was there looking for someone, and I found the tunnel just before the attack!" she replied between sobs.

Conor sat down next to her and put his arm around her. He knew she was telling the truth about what she had told him. He also felt that she was keeping something from him, a deep secret. He decided to just go ahead and ask her what it was. "Elizabeth, I believe you are holding on to a secret that you want to share. But you are afraid, and you don't know if you can trust me. I tell you now that, God as my witness, you can trust me. I like you very much and want to help!"

When he said that, she threw her arms around his neck and sobbed even more. When she stopped crying, she looked up at him. "I was in the village, trying to locate a group of very tiny people we believe live there."

Half joking he said, "More fairy tales?" but this time he was smiling.

She frowned at him and continued, "I was sent to England by the group of Tinys I care for in Ireland."

"Wait! There are more of them in Ireland?" he asked.

"Yes! My father was their benefactor for many years, as was his father and his before that. Because my father had no sons, it fell to me when he passed. When the war broke out, my little ones grew very concerned about the others that are living in England. I was asked to go and try to get them to come back to Ireland. I had told the villagers I was looking for an uncle, so as to not disclose my real task. Although it appeared the villagers knew of the little ones and were helping to hide and care for them. As I told you, I had just located the trap door to the tunnel when the attack came. I managed to get inside and crawl back about twenty feet, and that is when I found the little ones. They are still there, waiting for me to return and help them leave. Now do you believe me?"

"Yes, I believe you about the little ones, as you call them, a group of small people, but the part about a treasure"—Conor looked at the floor and with a sigh continued—"I just don't know."

"Why is that?" she asked.

"Well, I find it hard to believe that anyone big or small who had a fortune would choose to live in such a remote and backward place as that fishing village!" he explained.

She looked at him with a twinkle in her eye and said, "Not if you were afraid the Big people would harm you or take it away. You would hide in an out-of-the way place and do things like start a myth about leprechauns and fairies." Then she slowly and deliberately said, "Especially if you are only twelve inches tall!"

Conor was just sitting there with his eyes wide open. Then he softly said, "Twelve inches tall!"

The next morning the ship docked at Harwich. After morning muster and a quick check of the duty roster, Lieutenant O'Brien went to Elizabeth's cabin to see if she would like to get something to eat. He knocked on the door. When she opened it, he saw that she was dressed and ready for a new day.

"Good morning, Elizabeth! Would you join me for breakfast?" he said with a big grin on his face.

"I would be delighted!" she replied with a smile as big as his grin.

Just then, their joy of seeing each other was interrupted by an announcement over the loud speaker.

"Lieutenant O'Brien, report to the bridge!"

"I guess breakfast will have to wait. I'll be back as soon as I can. Of course, you may go on ahead if you like," he told her.

"No, I will wait here for you," she replied.

He headed up to the bridge, wondering what that was all about. He had been given leave of all his other duties in order to try to get to the bottom of the German attack. Now he was trying to think what he must tell the captain if he asked what he had found.

As he entered the bridge, he saw the captain talking to the same marine sergeant from the landing party. As he got closer he heard, "…and he was on deck watch when he saw him leave?"

"Yes, sir, at five thirty this morning," answered the marine.

"Very good, Sergeant, you have your orders; that will be all!" Then turning to Lieutenant O'Brien, he inquired, "O'Brien, did Lieutenant Hobart sleep in his bunk last night?"

"Why, I believe so, sir. I retired a bit late, but I thought I saw him sleeping when I came in? Why, what's the matter?"

"The matter is I have been informed that some things are missing from the ship. Money and even a pistol, so it appears we have a robbery on our hands," the captain explained.

"A robbery on one of Her Majesty's ships?" asked O'Brien.

"Yes, indeed, and that fool Lieutenant Hobart has gone missing without leave!" the captain further explained.

"AWOL, why that stupid…oh! Excuse me, sir!"

"That's quite all right, Lieutenant, I feel the same way. What a downright stupid thing to do. He should not have need of money. His father is well to do, you know!"

"Yes, sir, I know! But why did he do it?" asked the Lieutenant.

"That's what I wanted to ask you, Lieutenant. Do you have any idea what this might be all about?"

"Why, no sir, not off hand, other than he was upset about my putting him on report."

"Hmm, well you ask around, and see what you can find out," commanded the captain.

"Very good, sir!"

O'Brien saluted and started to leave when the captain asked, "Oh, by the way, did you uncover anything from talking to Miss O'Rourke? Anything that I might want to put in my report to the admiralty?"

"No, sir, I don't believe so, sir!" he answered, not wanting to give away Elizabeth's secret. But he knew he must tell the captain something. "A journal from one of the German officers described an incident where an English fisherman that was captured by them told a tail of lost treasure, and that's what they were searching for."

"A what? Treasure? Well, you can be sure I won't be telling tales of treasure in my report! That will be all, Lieutenant!"

"Aye, aye, sir!"

And the lieutenant left the bridge and almost ran to tell Elizabeth the news.

She was still waiting patiently in her room when he arrived and knocked on the door. As soon as she opened it, he rushed inside and closed it behind him. He took her hands in his and told all that went on and how he had told the captain about the treasure story and that the captain was dropping it from his reports. They hugged and kissed and then went to the dining room.

As they came to Conor's and Hobart's room, Conor stopped and said, "I think I had better go in and check to see if that rat took any of my money when he took off!"

He entered and went right to his locker and looked inside. He picked up the little box that he kept some odds and ends and a few dollars in, and, sure enough, the money was missing.

"Well, he cleaned me out!" he told Elizabeth, who was waiting in the passageway at the open door. He put the box back and closed the locker door and started to leave when he noticed something else was missing from his desk.

"The journal," he whispered. "*It's gone!*"

After finishing breakfast, Conor told Elizabeth that he had some leave time coming and that he would go to the captain and request it now that they were in port.

The captain looked up from reading the request form and said, "Off on a spot of leave, is it? Jolly good! And what of that Miss...what's her name?"

"Miss O'Rourke, sir!"

"Yes, yes of course, O'Rourke! From Ireland, as I recall!"

"Yes, sir! I'll be escorting her back to the village to see about getting some of her things."

"Very good, carry on!"

"Aye, sir!" And he was off on the run!

As they left the ship, Conor saw a fellow officer getting into a truck on the dock and called out, "Hey, Hartford, how's about giving us a lift to a decent restaurant!"

"Sure thing, Yank, hop in!" he replied. A few minutes later they were climbing out of the truck and saying thanks for the ride.

Conor turned to Elizabeth and said, "I will try to hire a car here. I don't think we will be able to find one once we get up the coast."

"All right, then I'll go to the deli there on the corner and pick up some sandwiches and things for the trip and meet you here when I'm done," Elizabeth said.

After two hours of trying everywhere, he failed to find anyone who had a car to let. He found Elizabeth sitting in the restaurant in a booth.

"Did you get a car?" she asked.

"I'm afraid not! There are so few cars around, and most of them are being used for the war effort."

"What will we do?" she asked.

"I've been thinking about that for some time, and I have a plan!" he said.

He plopped down beside her, and she said with a sigh of relief, "Good, what is it?"

"Okay! Here it is: we take the train to Newcastle, and then we hire a truck or a team and wagon, load up some supplies, and head for the Blyth."

She thought for a minute and then asked, "What about Hobart? Do you think he knows about the treasure, and maybe that's why he stole the journal and went missing?

"Yes! He must have read it or overheard us talking last night. He's just crazy enough to try to go there, so we must hurry!" Then he hesitated.

"What's wrong? What is it, Conor?"

"I'm a bit embarrassed. You see, I don't have very much money on me, and we don't get paid until a week from now."

"Oh! Don't worry, we have plenty of money, see!"

She reached into her pocket and pulled out a large roll of bills.

"Where in the world did you get that?" he asked.

"Well!" she said as she put the bills back in her pocket, "While I was out shopping, I noticed a little coin shop that was just across

the street, and it is owned by the nicest, little old man. I showed him some coins I had, and he got very excited and offered to buy them at a very reasonable price, so I sold some to him!"

"Coins? What coins?" he questioned.

"They were like these!" she said as she opened up her bag to reveal about thirty solid gold doubloons! She laughed at the look on his face and then got up and held out her hand and said, "Let's go catch that train, and on the trip I promise to tell you everything!"

"Everything?" he questioned as he got up. They walked out of the restaurant and headed to the train station.

Hidden Treasure

Lieutenant Hobart had managed to catch an earlier train and arrived in Newcastle hours ahead of Conor and Elizabeth. But he was unable to find a car or truck to drive to the village, so after considering for some time, he decided to call his father in London.

"Hobart residence!" the butler answered the phone in his usual dull tone.

"Jameson, this is Harry! I must speak to Father straight away!"

"I believe he is having his breakfast, young sir, and you know he cannot be disturbed at breakfast!"

"But this is an emergency. I must insist!" Hobart explained.

"Oh, very well, but you know he will be most angry with you!" Jameson said and went to tell his master that his son was on the telephone. When he entered the room where the senior Hobart was, he announced himself with, "Ah, hum, beg your pardon, sir, but young Harry is on the telephone, and he insists that he speak to you right away! I did tell him you were not to be disturbed, but…"

Hobart looked up over the morning paper, "What, Harry on the phone? You know I'm not to be bothered! Oh, very well, put him on!"

When the butler handed him the phone, he said, "Well, what is it now, Harry? I'm having breakfast, you know!"

"I'm sorry to disturb you, Father, but I need you to send our car and driver up to Newcastle right away!" Harry said.

"Newcastle? Whatever for?" his father asked.

"I'm stuck here, and I must get over to Blyth, and there are no cars to let here!"

"What the deuces are you doing in Newcastle? I thought you were on your ship, out to sea and all that!"

"Yes, sir, I was, but I left the ship…"

"You *what*? Harry, you can't just leave the ship! Are you on leave?"

"Well, no, sir, I just left!"

"You went absent without permission? Don't you know there is a war on? They could have you shot for that! You get back to that ship straight away! I will not have a Hobart shot for desertion, do you hear me?"

"But, Father, I must find the treasure!"

"Treasure? What nonsense are you talking about now? Now, you listen to me, young man…"

"But it's the treasure that Grandfather used to tell us about in his stories!" Harry insisted.

"Poppycock and fairy tales, that's what my father put into your head. Poppycock, I say!"

"But I found a journal!" Harry tried to explain.

"Now you listen to me, Harry, I'm sending my chauffer to fetch you and bring you back to your ship. Is that understood?" his father demanded.

All of the sudden, Harry Hobart got an idea! He would let his father think he would go back with the chauffer, and when he got there…

"All right, Father. I'll come back. Please send the car for me."

"Good, I'll have it sent up right away! By the by, where will he find you?" asked Hobart senior.

"I'll just wait here at the train station."

Harry said with a wicked grin on his face and his hand on the pistol, tucked into his belt and hidden under his coat.

Elizabeth and Conor were able to get tickets on the next train to Newcastle. On the train trip Elizabeth and Conor got to know more about each other. As each mile passed, they were beginning to fall in love.

She told him about how she cared for the little ones in Ireland, how long ago the little ones used some of their treasure to help their caretakers. Many companies were started, and now they had developed into a very large corporation called Hawk Enterprises. "With each new caretaker, the business is now passed on to them, and they become the head of Hawk Enterprises."

"Hawk is a funny name for a company. Where did that name come from?" Conor asked.

"The name was chosen to honor the two men who first helped the little ones. They were men of wealth, an English count named William Hawks and his son Edward. He and his father were responsible for finding the Tinys. After his father's death, Edward went on to care for and educate the Tinys. And with the Tinys' help, he founded Hawk and Company. I believe that was around the year sixteen fifty."

"Now, tell me more about you and your family," she said.

He leaned back in the seat and, taking her hand, said, "It all started long, long ago, when I was very young!" He laughed, and she smacked him on the arm. Then he turned serious. "My family is from the South. My father builds boats, fishing boats mostly, but we do make a few sea-going yachts. My grandfather and grandmother came to America in eighteen fifty. When they first married, they settled in South Carolina. He was also a boat builder."

"Where did your grandparents come from?" she asked.

"They came from Ireland. If I remember correctly, they were from a small fishing village near Dublin."

They spent all the remaining travel time telling each other about their families and themselves. By the time they finally reached Newcastle, they were happy and had almost forgotten all about Hobart—that is, until they stepped off the train.

As they entered the station, Conor saw Hobart. He was sitting across the room, facing away from them and had not seen them enter the station. Conor started to go over to him and tell him to go back to the ship and to turn himself in before he got into even more trouble. But before he could, things started to happen.

First, the chauffer arrived at the front of the station with the limousine. Then just as Hobart was about to confront the chauffer with the gun and force him to give him the car, another vehicle pulled up, and it had two marines in it.

Hobart had just come out of the station door when he saw the marine sergeant from the ship. He quickly pulled the pistol from his belt and fired, but he missed the sergeant and hit the corporal in the left arm.

The sergeant saw Hobart pull out the gun, and he returned fire and hit him in the leg, knocking him down and sending Hobart's pistol flying.

Conor, who was trying to get to Hobart and stop him, ran over and picked up the pistol.

Hobart was lying on the sidewalk, yelling and whining in pain and holding his wounded leg.

The sergeant, seeing Hobart was no longer armed, turned and saw to the corporal.

Meanwhile Elizabeth was trying to calm Hobart down and get his wound bandaged. When the sergeant finished dressing the corporal's arm, he came over to where Hobart was laying and saluted Conor. "Sir, I have orders to return this man to the ship!"

Conor handed him the gun and said, "Very good, Sergeant, carry on!"

"You and the miss will be okay?"

"Yes, Sergeant, we will be fine!" replied Conor.

Then he noticed the marines had arrived in a truck, and he got an idea!

"Sergeant, where did you get that lorry?"

"From the motor pool, sir!"

Conor took the sergeant by the arm and walked him over to the limo. "How would you and the corporal there like to ride back to the ship in that?" he asked as he pointed to the limo.

"Sir?"

"I don't believe either of you can drive that lorry. The corporal is wounded, and you have this dangerous prisoner that must be watched at all times. I'll commandeer that limo and the driver to take you back to the ship, and I will return the lorry myself."

The sergeant, by then, had caught on to what the lieutenant was suggesting and smiled and said, "Yes, sir, that would be most helpful!"

The sergeant, the corporal, and Hobart got into the limo, and they all drove off. Conor and Elizabeth took the truck and headed for the fishing village.

At the village it took some time to convince the Tinys, as Conor had decided to call them, that he was there to help. After getting a few of them to meet him and talk with him, they all came around. As Elizabeth watched how he talked to them, how he listened to what they had to say, and was concerned for their safety, she was becoming surer that this may be the man for her.

Once the Tinys had approved of their new member, they got to work gathering up all their belongings and anything else they could load on the truck, including several crates of "farm equipment."

Conor was so busy helping to load everything that at first he didn't take notice that each of the crates had a strong canvas bag attached to hooks screwed into the sides of the all four corners. And the bags were hanging by their straps with the bag up in

the air like they were filled with gas like a balloon, but they were not puffed out like a balloon. After twenty or so heavy crates, he finally asked, "Elizabeth, what in the world do they have in all these crates of farm equipment, and what's in the bags attached to them?"

Elizabeth motioned for the next crate in line to be put aside. The four Tinys that were carrying it lifted the crate up over their heads and just shoved it in the direction of the two big people. It floated through the air a few feet and then slowly settled to the ground. Conor went over to it and put his hand on one of the bags and pushed down. It took a lot more pressure than he thought it would, but he did get it to go down, and as it did, it felt like the bag was full of rocks.

"Be very careful and open one of the bags while it's floating there, and reach up inside…"

"No! Wait!" One of the Tinys yelled and came over, reached in his pocket, and pulled out a little red rock and handed it to Conor. As he put in Conor's hand, he said, "Careful, don't open your hand or it will fly up and away."

Conor just stood there with this little rock in his hand, not sure what to do after that stern warning.

Elizabeth came over and gently took the red rock out of his hand; she held her hand upside down and opened it. The rock stayed there and didn't fall like it was glued to her palm. Closing her hand, she looked around and then climbed up into the canvas-covered back of the army truck. She motioned for Conor to follow her, and when he got next to her, she held out her hand and let go of the red rock. It fell straight up to the canvas and stopped. Conor looked up at the rock and back at her. "You mean to tell me that those bags are all filled with red rocks."

"Yes, and that is how they can move those heavy boxes," she replied.

"But where did they come from, and how do they rise up like that?" he asked.

"They were found long ago in a cave, but I'm afraid we no longer know where that cave is. Its whereabouts have long been forgotten. As for how they do what they do, no one knows. It is a mystery."

"But look! This is what's inside the crates." Then she picked up a pry bar and opened one of the crates. Inside all he could see was straw until she moved the straw aside to revel several canvas sacks. "Open it!" she said with a grin.

He reached in and opened one and looked in to find gold coins, hundreds of gold coins like the ones she had in her bag back in Harwich. He whistled. "So, this is the treasure the Germans and Hobart were after!"

Elizabeth smiled and explained, "This is only a small part of the fortune that was given to the little ones by Count Hawks. Each of the two groups has a small amount they use to help those that help them. Like the villagers that were here," she said sadly.

"But like I told you on the trip up here, they have invested a great deal of the fortune in building the companies that make up Hawk Enterprises. Oh! And then there are the banks!" With that she smiled.

He sat down on one of the crates. "You mean to tell me they own banks?"

"But of course, where else would they keep most of their gold and silver?" she giggled.

One of the Tinys jumped into the crate, closed the sack, covered it back up, and climbed out as others closed the lid and re-nailed it shut. All Conor could say was "Wow, you guys work really fast!"

One of the Tiny men looked up at Conor and winked.

Conor stepped down from the truck, stood back, and for the first time took a good look at how these Tiny people all worked together to load the truck. They had put together a wooden path from the cave to the back of the truck. He could see that some of the wood was charred.

THE TELLING

They have used wood from the village to make the path and the ramp up to the truck, he thought to himself. As he investigates further, he saw there were no wheels under the crates and boxes that were being brought out of the cave. The things they were moving were simply floating in air by being lifted by the bags of red rocks. He just stood there in amazement, smiling.

Elizabeth, who had been directing most of this, came over to him. "What are you grinning about?"

He put his arm around her shoulders. "Oh, I was just watching them at work and how they manage to move all of those large crates. It's just so amazing to see!"

Having secured all the little ones in the truck along with their treasure and belongings, Conor and Elizabeth set out for Maryport on the west coast of England. There they would meet a ship for Ireland. Elizabeth had planned their whole journey. While they were in Newcastle, she made all the arrangements with a company they owned to have a cargo ship waiting for them in Maryport.

Once they were on the road, a lot of the Tinys came into the cab of the truck to talk with Conor. They all seemed very interested in the fact that he was from America. They asked him many questions about where he lived and his family. He was enjoying answering their questions and talking to them.

As they talked and asked questions, he saw these people had such a lust for life and knowledge. To his surprise, they were all very well educated.

After things had been quiet for a while, he turned to Elizabeth, who was in the passenger's seat. "They really love to learn, don't they?"

"Yes! I have found that they have some of the brightest minds of anyone I have ever met. I consult with them, and they help me with company decisions all the time."

The eldest Tiny, the one Elizabeth met in the cave, came up to the cab to sit and watch Conor drive. After a while he asked, "Is it hard to learn to use your hands and feet to move those pedals and the steering wheel and the levers all at the same time?"

Conor, who had been going through the gears as they climbed some hills, said, "No, not really, but it does take a bit of practice to be good at it!"

"Why do you need to be good at it?" asked the old one.

Conor smiled and answered, "You need to be able to coordinate the moving of the gears in order to make the truck move smoothly and safely."

"Ah! I see," the old one said. Then he sat silently and just watched for a few miles.

As the trip progressed, the Tinys asked Elizabeth to come back to talk with them.

The old man asked, "Elizabeth, you have taken care of our brothers and sisters in Ireland for over five years now. Isn't that correct?"

"Yes, that's right. Ever since my father passed, I have cared for them. Why do you ask?"

He looked around at the others, and they all encouraged him to continue, "Well, we have been talking. We really like you and Conor!" He paused for a second. "We were wondering if you would be our caretaker as well?"

And from the group come many yeses and yeahs.

Elizabeth smiled and said, "But of course. When we get to Ireland, I will take care of you too!"

Now she heard a lot of nos and not theres out of the group.

She was puzzled and said, "I don't understand? What's wrong?"

And all of them at the same time said, "America, we want to go to America!"

She was taken aback and said, "I can't take you to America!"

Then the old man said with a smile, "You can! If you go with Conor!"

They all yelled, "Go with Conor, go with Conor!" and started laughing.

So, by the time they reached Maryport things had changed! Elizabeth directed Conor to the warehouse owned by Hawk Enterprises. Once they were safely inside and the door closed, the Tinys all started talking to her very excitedly. Conor got out of the truck and walked around to the back to see what that was all about.

"What's all the fuss?" he asked as he opened up the back so that they could get out.

Elizabeth climbed down and looked back at all the anxious faces, shrugged her shoulders, and said, "They all have decided that they don't want to go to Ireland to live."

"They don't? Don't tell me they want to go back?" he said.

"No! They don't want to live in England either!"

He looked at all the faces that were smiling at him. They looked like they were about to burst with anticipation. "Okay, so where do they want to live?" he asked.

All of them yelled, "In *America* with *you* and *Elizabeth*!" Then they all laughed in unison. It was decided that they would stay in Ireland until the war ended, as it would be far too dangerous to try to go to America now that the Americans had joined the fight against Germany. They did not realize it would be two more years before the war would end.

Conor helped get the Tinys settled in Ireland, and then he had to return to his ship. Over the next two years, he did manage, as often as he could get leave, to come see Elizabeth and visit with the Tinys. After about a year of visits, Conor did ask Elizabeth to marry him. Of course, she said yes, but they agreed to wait until the war was over and he was discharged.

Conor heard that Harry Hobart was charged with leaving his post without permission. The charges for shooting the corporal

somehow got dropped after the corporal mysteriously came into a large sum of money. The last Conor heard was that Hobart's father had bought Harry's way out of the navy and all the trouble he was in. Conor doubted that would last very long.

WWI finally ended in 1919. Shortly thereafter, Conor was discharged from the British Navy. Elizabeth and Conor were married a month later. When they got ready to come to America, some of the Tinys wanted to stay in Ireland. So after finding one of Elizabeth's male cousins to care for the Irish Tinys, they brought about half of the Tinys to America.

They lived in South Carolina for a few years, but finally moved and settled here in Tennessee.

Vaughn said, "The end," then closed and put down the book of telling.

One of the children raised a hand.

"Yes, what is it?" asked Vaughn.

"Was Conor and Elizabeth our Conor's great- grandfather and grandmother?

"No, they were his great-great-grandparents."

With no more questions from the teenagers, Vaughn took the book and returned to his seat. Graybeard then got up, went to the podium, and raised his hands to quiet everyone. When he saw that the kids had settled down, he said, "Let us close the telling with a prayer." Lowering his head, he began, "Heavenly Father, as we gather together to celebrate another telling of our history, we give thanks to you for the O'Briens and now Janet and Brittany who has joined them in helping to keep us safe here in Tennessee. We ask that you bless those that bless us and forgive those that would do us harm. Everything else we leave in your hands. Amen!"

Looking up, he shouted, "*Now, let's eat and have some fun!*"

The Hobarts

Present Day England

    The headquarters for Hobart Industries, Ltd. was based in London, England; the massive building complex covered a quarter of a mile. The main office building, where the president and CEO, Randle L. Hobart, had his office, is a ten-story giant. His office alone occupied over a quarter of the top floor. It held some of the most expensive furniture and artifacts to be found in the world. Randle was young, in his early twenties, his brown hair along with his manicured nails were perfectly groomed. He wore a suit that looked like it cost more than most people make in a month. There always seemed to be an air of superiority about him.

    His secretary announced over the intercom, "Sir, you have a call on line two."

    "Who is it?" he asked very gruffly.

    "It's Mr. Simms of Simms shipping," she answers.

    "Simms! Good, put him through," he replied rubbing his hands together like he was going to get something he always wanted. "Hello, is that you, Simms?" he asked smoothly, knowing it was.

    "Yes, it's me! Now you listen here, Hobart! You can't get away with this sort of thing!"

    "Why, Simms, what are you talking about?" Hobart inquired with a grin on his face.

    "You know good and well what I'm talking about!" Simms yelled. "You can't do this to me! I made a deal with your father. You can't just stop supplying us overnight. This is outrageous!"

"I can, and I will if you don't take my offer," Hobart said hatefully.

"Why you little cheat. Just because my son caught you cheating in college…" Simms started.

"Look, Simms, you have a choice: your yacht or your company! Make up your mind. Now!"

"Oh all right you can have the yacht, and at your price, but you will live to regret this, Hobart. Mark my words!" Simms said, giving in to Hobart's blackmail and slamming down the phone.

Outside the office his secretary could hear Hobart laughing like a madman. Reaching down, she turned off the recorder hidden in her desk.

Later that day, sitting behind his enormous desk, Randle Hobart was talking on the phone.

"I don't care what you have to do, or who you have to do it too. I want controlling interest in that company *today!*" He slammed the phone down and yelled, "How I hate incompetents! Why can't I find employees with brains?"

He got up from behind his desk and started pacing around the room thinking to himself.

Why did you have to go and die without telling me about them?

Randle sat once more behind his desk and thought about all that had happen in the last three years. His father had died of a heart attack, and he had been called home from college to assume control of the family business. He had just started to flex his corporate muscle in the last six months, and he liked it. The power and control he had over others was intoxicating. Hobart Industries was one of the largest holding companies in the world. It had its hands in commercial airlines, shipping, oil, and mining, just to name a few. If it was a multi-million dollar company, you could bet Hobart Industries held stock in it!

Randle started thinking back to the last time he had spoken to his father. He had been home from collage at his family's estate in England. The conversation he had with his father ran through his mind.

"Well, got caught cheating again, did you?" his father asked.

The fact that he had been asked to leave three of the top universities in the country had not set well with Dad.

"It was my roommate, he turned me in, the dirty…"

"So, what are you going to do now?" his father interrupted.

"I am going to fix him for good!" Randle replied.

"No, no! I meant about finishing school! I could care less about what you do to whoever it was! Or how you do it! But you will finish college. Is that clear?"

"How can I turn over the company to you if you can't even finish college?"

"School is boring! Why do I need to finish? You control the company and can do whatever you want! If you say I'm in, the board will have to allow it!" replied Randle.

"Sure I could do that, but it's not the board that I'm worried about. There's someone higher up that worries me!" his father announced.

"Higher up than you? How can that be? You own the company!"

"Son, I manage the company."

"I guess it's time I told you. I was waiting until you finished college and you were ready to take over, but now is as good a time as any."

And then the next words his father had said burned in his memory.

"It's your aunt that holds total, unyielding control of Hobart Industries; I'm nothing more than a puppet!"

And now, Randle thought, I'm that puppet!

His private phone ringing brought him out of his thoughts with a start.

"What?" he yelled as he answered it.

The calm voice of his secretary was on the other end of the line. "Your aunt is on line one, sir."

"What! No! I can't talk to her right now! Uh…tell her I'm out of the office!"

"Yes, sir!" Miss Baryl replied and then clicked back to talk to his aunt. "I'm sorry, Mrs. Hobart, but Mr. Hobart seems to be out of the office, may I take a message?"

"Out is he? Well you give him this message: I will be in London on the thirteenth, and I expect to see some results!" Then she hung up.

The intercom on her desk buzzed, and she answers. "Yes, Mr. Hobart?"

"What did she say?" he asked, sounding like a schoolboy that knows he is in trouble.

Miss Baryl gave him the message. Without even acknowledging her, he just clicked off. She muttered to herself, "And I thought your father was hard to work for. But you, young Mr. Power Hungry, take the prize!"

Later that day, while going through some of his father's old files, he came across an old key. He called his secretary.

"Miss Baryl, I need to see you."

As she enters the office he held up the key. "Have you seen this before?"

"Yes, sir," she answered, after taking a closer look at it.

"Do you know what it's for?" he asked.

"I do believe it's for the old box your father kept in his secret safe."

"Secret safe? What secret safe?"

"The one hidden in the underside of your desk, sir."

"I didn't know… Why hadn't you informed me of it?" he asked, starting to get angry.

"You never asked, sir," she replies with a slight smirk in her voice. "Will that be all, sir?"

By now he has turned his attention to the desk. "Yes! Yes! Go!" He said as he waved his arm at the door. "Call maintenance, and have someone come up to move this desk," he ordered, still looking at the huge, wooden desk his father had used every day. "No, wait! I will do it myself!" he said, changing his mind not wanting anyone knowing the location of the safe.

She turned again to leave wanting to get back to her own desk. He stopped her with yet another question, "Who else knows of the safe?"

She turned back to face him and replied, "Now that your father has passed, only you and I, sir"

"Good! That will be all!" he said with another dismissing wave.

As he studied the finely carved, wooden desk, he wondered if he could indeed move it. "Why, this thing must weigh five hundred pounds!" he exclaimed as he walked around it, looking at the floor trying to see where the safe was. "Hmmm, no seams or cracks that I can see? Where could it be?"

Getting down on his hands and knees, he crawled around under the huge desk, tapping here and there to see if he could determine where there might be a hollow place. After about five minutes of crawling and tapping, he got up and moved around to his chair. After sitting down in disgust, he reached over and hit the intercom button to call Miss Baryl.

"Yes, sir?" came her quick but exasperated reply.

"Miss Baryl, would you come in here please."

"Right away, sir"

Upon entering his office, she crossed the room to stand in front of his desk.

"Are you sure the safe in the floor is under the desk?" he questioned.

"No, sir"

"What?" he yelled. "But you just said it was under the desk"

"Sir, I simply said it was under the desk. I did not say it was in the floor."

"Oh! Okay," he exclaimed, more interested in finding the safe and its contents than reprimanding her for not explaining the whereabouts in the first place.

"Very well then, that will be all." And again she was dismissed.

By the time she closed the door, his attention was fully back on the desk. He knelt down and looked underneath but saw nothing to indicate a safe. Sitting back down in his chair, he glared at this monster of a desk and turned the key over and over in his hand.

"Where could it be?"

He liked a good puzzle, but was growing tired of this one.

"This key fits a lock to a safe," he said to himself as he held up the key. It was then he noticed the inscription on the key; it read, "If one were blind of nine that see, a mystery solved, to use the key."

"If one were blind?" he repeated out loud. "One what?"

He moved his chair farther back from the desk so he could see under it better. Reading the words on the key once more, he said, "One of nine; nine that see? See what?" He repeated, "Nine that see," over and over while studying the desk. Then his attention fell on one of the massive legs. There he saw three carved lion heads.

"Hmm...three carved heads per leg, times four, no wait, there are only three legs. Why hadn't I noticed that before?" There were two legs on his side of the desk but only one centered in the front. *Very strange design.* he thought.

"Three legs, times three heads that worked out to be nine heads. The nine that see!"

Kneeling once again, he examined each leg and the nine lion heads.

"Now which one is blind?"

He looked carefully at each face only to find that all of them had their eyes open, and none appeared to be different from the rest.

"How can only one be blind if they are all the same?"

Sitting there scratching his head, he said, "How did that inscription go? If one were blind of nine that see, something, something?"

As he sat there looking from face to face, he wondered out loud, "Of nine that see? How do you make one of these wooden faces not see? Poke them in the eye? Ha!"

He laughed at his own joke then suddenly stopped. "Could that be it? You have to push on an eye or something like that." Sensing he was on the right track, he moved from leg to leg, pushing on one eye after another but to no avail. He was by now becoming more and more frustrated, yet at the same time more determined to find the answer and the secret safe.

"It has to be something to do with lions eyes," he said out loud. "Do you cover them up? No, I don't see any electric eyes in them. I tried pushing each eye, and that didn't work. Wait a minute…you can't make one blind by poking just one eye. You need to poke both of them!"

With this new revelation, he returned to the faces and started pushing both eyes on each leg. First the leg to the right of center, nothing happened. Then the left of center again; nothing. Finally he tried the center leg. *Click!* The eyes retracted into the leg at the same time a panel opened up in the bottom of the desk. The opening revealed a small safe with a lock that looked as if the key would fit. Upon trying the key, he found that it did indeed fit. He turned it, and the safe opened.

Inside the safe he found a leather-covered box. Inside was a note from his father. The note read,

> Contained in this box are the clues to finding a secret. The ledger tells of how it was found and lost many years ago when it was stolen from our forefathers. The records of the

search for them and the many failures over the years have been written in this ledger. I feel that I was very close to finding them after searching for over fifty years. But now with my health failing, I leave this ledger and the journal to help in your search. Guard it well, for no one knows of it or the secret we seek. If you succeed in finding them, they will bring you fame and fortune.

"Secrets and lost fortunes! Now we're getting somewhere!"

He turned the ledger over in his hands, checking out the designs engraved in the old book. On the outer cover, he recognized the family crest. Inscribed under the crest was another rhyme: "A secret lost, a tiny thing, when found again, will riches bring."

He remembered his grandfather's tales of mystery and treasure. The stories of how their ancestors had found and lost a great treasure. Down through the years, each new generation would take up the hunt, but they had never found it again! Now that's what he wanted to do, take up the hunt!

"The hunt for what?" he asked himself. "I don't even know what Grandfather was talking about."

He only knew that as a young lad, the stories had intrigued him and captured his imagination. He picked up the journal and noticed that it had an iron cross on the front. He opened it to find that it is written in German, and he saw a date in the upper-right corner of the first page that read, "1917, 12, Oktober."

"Nineteen seventeen?" He said to himself. "Why, that was clear back in World War One!" As he tried to read more, he slammed it shut. "German! I wish I had paid attention in that class! I need someone who can read this for me. *No!* Wait! I will have to do it myself. I don't want anyone else seeing this!"

He turned his attention to the ledger just as his private line rang. Still reading the ledger, he answered distractedly, "Yes?"

"Your aunt again, sir, she insists that she talk to you immediately," Miss Baryl said.

"Very well," Randle answered calmly, "put her through." The phone clicked and Randle said, "Aunt Matilda, it's good to hear from you. How are you feeling? Well, I hope!"

"*Randle!*" she shouted. "What are you up to? I have been trying to get through to you for three days! I want some answers, and I mean now!"

Smiling to himself, Randle replied, "I'm so sorry we have been missing each other, but you know how busy it is around here. Oh, by the way, I found it!"

"Listen to me, Randle, if you ever…" She stopped and then said, "Found it. Found what? Are you saying that you found your father's ledger? Randle, do not play with me!"

"*No, no*! Aunty, you see I found it just now. I also found a journal from World War One, but it's in German!"

"Don't say anything more over the phones. I will be there as soon as I can!" she said.

"Yes, Aunt Matilda. I look forward to seeing you!" he lied.

At the station, the train came to a stop. Parked nearby was a big black limo. Randle Hobart got out and came over to meet his aunt at her private railroad car.

"Good morning, Aunty!" he said, "How was your trip?"

"Awful, just awful!" she replied grumpily as she slowly stepped down from the rail car.

"This thing sways and clanks so; a body can't even get a night's sleep!"

Randle, taking her hand to help her down said, "Why don't you use one of our jets? They're much faster and a lot quieter."

She looked at him with a scowl. "Now, Randle, you know I hate airplanes! Ever since your grandfather was shot down and killed in nineteen thirty-nine, I just don't trust them. No, not at all!"

The trip to Hobart headquarters was quiet, mostly because his aunt fell asleep on the way into town. Randle was very anxious to show his aunt what he found, hoping that once she saw it, she would get off his back for a while.

Randle was trying to figure out how to find out what the German journal had to do with the treasure his father was talking about in his notes. When the private elevator arrived at Randle's outer office, Miss Baryl was there, busily typing away on her computer. She looked to see the elevator doors slide open, and out came Randle and an elderly woman. The wheelchair she was in was being pushed by her chauffer. She looked to be in her eighties and was dressed in fine clothes and jewelry. Upon seeing the aunt, she thought to herself, *Oh no, not her again! I thought the kid was bad enough until she started coming around after Randle's father died.* And as the two Hobarts approached, she stood and greeted them.

"Good morning, Mrs. Hobart, Mr. Hobart!"

As they enter his office, Randle announced, "We do not want to be disturbed!" Then he abruptly shut the door.

Once inside, Aunt Matilda started asking questions. "Well, what have you learned so far? Have you translated the journal? And what of the little ones your father talked about? I just want to see a little one for myself!"

As Randle sat down behind his large desk, her chauffer parked his aunt's chair nearby.

"I will try to answer all you questions, but what about him?" he said and nodded at the chauffer.

She turned to look at her chauffer. "Never mind him! Get on with it."

Randle hesitated. "But Aunty?"

"Oh! All right!" she conceded. "Jameson, wait outside."

"Yes, madam," and he left.

Now that it was just the two of them, Randle continued, "I haven't had much time. You know those stories about the little ones are just that, stories! Aunty, that's all!"

"No, they are not just stories, and stop calling me Aunty. I hate that! Do you hear me?"

"Yes, Aunt Matilda, but father never found any real proof that they exist."

"What about the German's journal? What information did you find in it?"

"I don't know. I have not been able to read it," he answered.

"And what are you doing about it? Are you going to translate it yourself?" his aunt pressed him.

"No!" he replied. "I had Miss Baryl buy a program that will do that, and when she has it all done…"

"*You did what?*" his aunt screamed. "Are you out of your mind? Now she will know all about our secret! You idiot!"

Hobart shrank behind his desk and tried to calm her down. "But, Aunt Matilda, she has been with this company all these years and was very loyal to father!"

"I don't trust her or anyone else! As soon as she has the translation finished, I want her gone! Do you understand me?" she demanded.

"Yes, Aunt Matilda."

"Send Jameson back in!"

He came in and started to push the wheelchair out of his office. At the door she turned around. "Remember, nephew, I hold the power! And you, just like your father, are merely the puppet head of this company." With that she left

Miss Baryl had been listening to all this from her desk, as she had done so many times before.

No one knew that many years ago she had placed a secret microphone in the ceiling just above the big desk. She had rigged it so that it worked through the same earphones she used when typing the boss's dictations.

As she heard all this, she thought to herself, *Why in the world is this group of dwarfs so important to them? Somehow I must find out what this is all about! I must protect myself from her!* She quickly finished interpreting the German journal.

It had been weeks since Randle put in place a full worldwide search for the little ones and the treasure. In his office he was yelling on the phone at one of his operatives, "I want them found! I will not explain how important this is to you again! If you don't find them for me, and soon, I will see to it that something happens to you! And it will be a permanent something! Do I make myself clear?" With that he slammed the phone down and cursed.

Just then the door to his office opened, and in rolled his Aunt, unannounced. Her chauffer pushed her in front of Randle's big desk, locked the breaks on her wheelchair, tipped his hat, then promptly left the office.

"Well, Randle, I see you're in a fine mood. Do we have any results yet?" she asked.

"I was just about to call you," he lied. "We are making some progress, Aunt!"

His face had gone pale, and his voice was shaky.

"Randle, some progress is not what I want to hear. You are my nephew, and I love you, but if you do not find them in short order, all the power and finances of Hobart enterprises will be stripped from you. I will bring you down to nothing!" she said, her voice filled with anger and distaste. "I will destroy you and see to it that the memory of your name is forgotten forever!"

The last words she yelled as she slammed her fist down hard on the arm of her wheelchair. Her eyes that were glaring red, along with the tone of her voice, suddenly went soft, and she continued, "Sweet heart, always remember that I am the *real power* behind the Hobart name. I am sure that with more money and resources than most small countries at your disposal, you can find

anyone in the world, let alone a clan of small people! Do not let your aunt down, nephew. That would not be wise! Do you understand, sweetie?" The last words were delivered with a smile.

"Yes, Aunt Matilda," he stuttered. "Let me bring you up to date." He cleared his throat and continued, "We have six agents. Here, let me show you!" He reached in one of the desk drawers and pushed a button. A panel on the wall across from his desk opened up to reveal a large monitor that displayed a map. He arose from his chair and went over to the monitor and pointed at the map. "Two are in Florida and one is in Kentucky. We have narrowed the search in the US to the southern states. I have three of my best men in Ireland who are following up on some very promising leads."

"Randle," his Aunt interrupted, "I do not care how many people you use. I only want results and quickly, dear!" With that she pushed a button on her wheelchair. Her chauffer returned, released the brakes, turned her around, and headed for the elevator.

Before the door closed, she added, "Remember, Randle, if you don't find them, and I don't get to see them with my own eyes before I die, you lose everything! *Everything*!" Her last words sent a chill down Randle's spine, and the door slid closed with a sinister hiss.

Miss Baryl heard Randle talking out loud to himself, "I'm a puppet, am I? I'll show her, the dried up old windbag!"

She heard him going through the draws in his father's old desk. He was opening and closing them and then ruffling through papers. Then it got very quiet, and in a low voice, he said, "I must get rid of her, but how? She has things set up so that if she doesn't give the go ahead to the board of directors before she dies, I lose it all! Curse her! If only I can find them and keep them from her, I could get her to give me the okay! Yeah, I can blackmail her by holding them back from her! I must find them!"

Just then Randle's private phone rang. He answered, "Yes! What do you have for me? Who? Wait tell me her name again,

Katelyn O'Rourke? Okay, I got that, what about her? Yeah, you think she is a descendent of whom? Oh! Elizabeth O'Rourke? How did you arrive at that? By tracing Elizabeth's family tree. You went to one of those websites and found her there. You blundering idiot, those things are phony! What? Okay! Go ahead and look into it, but I need results fast, and I mean *now*! Put a tail on her, and see where that leads us."

Trust

Miss Baryl, after hearing all this, decided to try to contact Katelyn O'Rourke. Finally she was going to find out what this was all about. That evening, locating Katelyn's phone number, she went to a payphone and called her.

"Hello, is this Katelyn O'Rourke?"

"Yes, may I ask who is calling?" Katelyn inquired.

"You don't know me, Miss O'Rourke, but I must see you in person. It's of vital importance!"

"I'm sorry, who is this?" Katelyn questioned.

"My name is Heather Baryl, and I fear you are in grave danger!"

"Danger? Whatever from?"

"Please, Miss O'Rourke! I must talk to you in person! Can we meet?"

"I don't know what this is all about, but I suppose we could meet at my home. Here, I'll give you my address."

"No! We must not meet there! I believe you're being followed!"

"Followed? By who?"

Now Katelyn was very frightened and thought she knew what this was all about. But she must play dumb and try to get as much information as she could.

"We must meet in secret, and you must make sure you are not followed!" Heather said.

"Wait! Is this a joke? Am I on the radio or something?" Katelyn asked, playing along.

"No! I assure you this is not a joke! Now can we at least meet and let me explain?"

"Okay, then if I assume you are telling me the truth and this is not a joke, what is it you want from me?" Katelyn asked.

Heather, seeing that this was not going to be as easy as she assumed, tried to calm down so she could convince Katelyn she was telling the truth. She said, "We can meet in a public place like a park or at the mall, wherever you feel is best! But I want you to take precautions. Go there in a very roundabout way, so as to lose anyone that might be following you. Do you understand?"

Katelyn asked, "Who are you? Do I know you?"

"No, you do not know me. We have never met, but I have knowledge of a secret that others are trying to uncover, and I believe that their search for that secret may put you in harm's way."

"Secret? What secret?" questioned Katelyn.

"Please, Katelyn, I cannot say any more over the phone! Will you meet me?"

Katelyn, hearing the distress in the woman's voice, decided to meet her. "Yes, I will! When and where?"

"Okay! First you pick where, and then we can work out how to go about it!"

They talked about meeting in a park that was about half way between Katelyn's house and where Heather said she lived. Then Heather gave her a few things to look for to see if anyone was following her. Next they planned a route with several stops at shops and a movie so that Katelyn could be sure she wasn't followed. Finally the last thing they set was the time to meet, 4:15 p.m. the following day.

Heather Baryl had called in to work saying she had forgotten a doctor's appointment and would be out all afternoon. Randle Hobart was not going to be in the office anyway, so she did not need to have anyone cover for her.

She also went through a routine to make sure she wasn't followed. She arrived at the park right at 4:12 p.m. She drove around twice before deciding where to park. As she pulled in, she noticed

a young lady with flaming-red hair, sitting in a car two spaces over and assumed it must be Katelyn.

She was shaking with fright as she got out of her car and walked over to Katelyn's.

Katelyn saw her get out, and as she approached, Katelyn rolled down the window just a little. Not knowing what to expect, she was ready to drive off quickly.

Miss Baryl stopped near the front of Katelyn's car.

"Miss O'Rourke?" she asked.

"Yes! Are you Heather Baryl?" Katelyn answered.

"Yes! Please, can we walk in the park?"

Katelyn was greatly relieved that this little lady in her mid-fifties with graying hair pulled back in a bun didn't look threatening at all. She decided that it would be all right to go with her and got out of the car. They started walking.

"What is this all about, Miss Baryl?"

Heather looked at Katelyn as they walk and thought to herself, *Well, you've come this far, you might as well tell her all you know!*

She took a breath and said, "What I'm about to tell you will most likely shock you. After years of loyal service, I am about to betray my employer. Even though I might lose everything just by contacting you, I must tell you what I know!"

As they walked a little farther, they came to a bench, which was located near the center of the park. Katelyn, seeing that the woman was obviously under a lot of stress, suggested that they sit down. "Why don't we sit here, and you can tell me what you know."

"All right," Heather said.

As they sat down, Katelyn noticed how pale and shaken Heather was. Hoping to relieve some of her fear, Katelyn began softly, "Please tell me what this is all about, and maybe I can help you?"

Heather started to cry. "I have worked for the Hobarts for twenty-nine years. I have known of some terrible things they

have done to get ahead in their business. However, I have always just turned my head and done my job!" She sniffed and reached in her purse and got out a hanky. Dabbing at her nose, she continued, "But when I learned of what they were up to with the little ones, I couldn't stay still anymore!"

"The little ones?" Katelyn asked, trying to act like she didn't understand what Heather was talking about.

Now the look on Heather's face became harder as she further added, "Katelyn, I have read the journal from the German officer in World War One. I know who you are and who your uncle is as well! So don't play dumb! I will most likely lose my retirement over this, and I didn't come here to play silly games. I know of the little people in Ireland and of the treasure that they hold!"

Now Katelyn knew for sure that this lady was telling the truth. "What is it then that you want of me?"

Heather looked up at her. "I don't want anything from you! What I want is to stop them from getting their grimy hands on those little ones and to help keep you and your uncle safe, if I can!"

Trouble in Ireland

A few days later, somewhere deep in a forest in Ireland, Michael had been running full out when he tripped over a tree root, sending his twelve-inch frame sprawling. Slowly he sat up and carefully took inventory, dusting himself off as he did. "Nothing broken," he said to himself as he rubbed his skinned knee. "Better slow down before I do break something!" he chided. "I must get back to the village quickly, but in one piece."

It was nighttime and very dark in the forest, too dark to be running, and he knew it. But the news he carried was so bad he had forgotten about the danger in his haste to get back. He limped a little as he started out again, slower this time, but he still was moving at a trot.

"Lord, guide my feet this night" was the small prayer he spoke aloud.

Back in the hills, Shawn Dugan was standing just outside the entrance to the little cave they only recently had to move into and had now called home. As the elder of the village, he was worried. It was both his nature and his job to worry. He could worry over the smallest things, but this night his concerns were of the larger size: the safety of his people!

It had been well over a month since his last contact with their benefactor, Thomas O'Rourke. Shawn and Thomas had been friends for many years now. He knew Thomas to be the kind of person who was always on time. So when he failed to show up at the normal time and place for their monthly meeting a week ago, he worried.

Shawn had sent Mike Dugan, his grandson and the village hunter, to find out what was wrong. Now Mike was late in returning, and of course Shawn was worried.

"Mike is our best, and if he doesn't return, I don't know what to do next!" Shawn said to himself as he looked out into the darkness of the night, hoping to see Mike.

His thoughts were about the people that were in his care. "We must leave this place, that's for sure, but where to go?" he asked out loud.

"You are going to come in out of the cool night, that's where you're going, Shawn Dugan."

Shawn turned to see his wife standing in the entrance to the cave.

In the forest, as Michael ran, he thought back, going over the events of the last two days.

It had taken him at least twenty-four hours to reach the home of Thomas O'Rourke. When he finally arrived, it was growing dark. Knowing that some of the Bigs had dogs for pets, Mike approached the back of the house with great caution and stealth.

He had to get past the house next to O'Rourke's. Just as he got about halfway there, he heard a dog coming around to the backyard. Michael dropped flat on the ground, hoping the dog hadn't seen him.

The dog came around the corner and moved to the center of the yard. This entire time Mike had been trying to see if the

dog was coming at him, but the grass was too high where he was lying. He decided to stay flat in hopes he wasn't seen.

The dog sniffed the air, sat down, and scratched the back of his ear with his hind leg. Then it stood up and went toward the house. He stopped at a pan of water near the faucet.

Mike heard the dog drinking and took advantage of the distraction to move quietly to the nearest tree. From behind the tree, he sneaked a peek and said, "No dog!" Mike panicked.

"Did he see me move? Where is he? Is he coming after me?"

Mike tried to get a grip on himself and listened to see if he could hear the dog coming his way, but there was nothing. All he could hear was the slight breeze blowing through the tree.

"Where is the dog? I must find out. Must not freeze. I must move *now*."

Forcing himself to move, he peeked around the side of the tree.

"No dog?"

Just then he heard the dog barking from in front of the house. Mike scrambled up the tree out of harm's way.

Resting safely up in the tree, Mike took the time to scan the area and get his bearings. "Now, the dog is in the front yard of the neighbor's house. The O'Rourke house is on the right." With the eyes of a skilled hunter, he slowly took in the terrain before him. He stopped and stared as he saw a picture through the window of the neighbor's house. The picture was moving.

"Oh, yeah." He remembered some of the hunters talking about how the Bigs had boxes that they called TVs. He watched for a while and saw a scene where a man fell down and was hurt. Then a young boy picked up a phone, dialed 911, and help arrived. Mike took another look around. Seeing that it was clear, he climbed down and moved toward the O'Rourke house.

He halted at the edge of the yard and removed a piece of paper from his small pocket. On it was written instructions on

how to get inside the O'Rourke house. After reading them again, he folded up the paper and put it away.

"Before I go in, I want to take a look around!" Carefully moving closer to the house, he headed around the right side to the front to check it first. But as he rounded the corner of the house, he stopped short. Parked in front of the house with three men sitting inside was a large, black vehicle.

Mike was hidden behind a bush and knew they could not see him. He decided to wait there for a few minutes to see if they were staying or leaving.

Mike heard one of the men say, "He's not answering his phone. What do you want us to do now?"

"No, sir!" The man talking turned his head to reveal the cell phone he was holding to his ear, and he continued to talk. "Yes, sir, we talked to him yesterday and told him what you said we should say.... No, sir, all the lights are out. We know he's in there, because Dick saw him through a window, and he was asleep in his bed.... Mr. Hobart, are you sure he's the one you've been looking for?... No, sir, as far as we can find out, he lives alone. There is a niece who lives in London. All the information we have said she was his only living relative.... No, sir, we have not seen her. We got the information using the bugging device I told you we put on his window.... Sir, he sure doesn't live like a man with millions of dollars.... Yes, sir, as soon as it gets dark, we will talk to him again. I will…"

Just then a police patrol car came around the corner.

The man quickly said, "Police, I'll call you back!" and hung up.

As the police started down the street, Dick, who was on the phone, told Tom behind the wheel, "Start up, and slowly drive away. Get us out of here!"

They left. Mike saw them drive around the corner and out of sight. Meanwhile the police car continued on down the street.

Mike went on around to the other side of the house and found the side door. As he got nearer, he spotted the doggy door in it.

He knew that Shawn told him that Mr. O'Rourke didn't have a dog, but he was still very weary when he saw that small door.

"Come on!" he told himself. "Get a grip on your nerves, and get in there before those guys decide to come back."

Then he spotted the dog dish sitting on the step. After a closer look, he realized that it was empty except for some old, dried-up leaves and a lot of dust.

Dust! he thought to himself. *So he really doesn't have a dog!*

Now he felt it was safe to enter through the doggy door. Ever so slowly, he pushed on it to see if it moved, and it did! He pushed harder. It opened wide, and in he went.

Inside he found a whole different world than he was used to. All the things in there were big, built for Big people. To him it all looked like he had just entered the home of a giant. But this giant was their friend and benefactor.

After taking a few seconds to get his bearings, Mike headed for the room he thought was the bedroom. Entering the bedroom, he walked over to the bed where Thomas O'Rourke was lying.

"Looks like he's sleeping. I must warn him about the men I saw outside!" Mike whispered to himself.

He looked around for a way to get up on the bed. Not finding anything to climb on, Mike went over to the bed, grabbed hold of the bed covers, and started to pull himself up.

Just then Mr. O'Rourke woke with a start. "What, who's there?" he exclaimed, and he tried to sit up. But he was very weak and could only get up on one elbow. As he was rubbing his eyes, he saw Mike finally get up onto the foot of his bed.

Mike removed his hat and said, "I'm sorry to have given you a start, Mr. O'Rourke, but I had to warn you!"

"Warn me? Of what?" replied O'Rourke.

Mike came a little closer so that the elderly man could hear him better.

"When I was outside, I saw three men in a black car. One of them was talking to someone on the phone!"

THE TELLING

O'Rourke's eyes opened wide, and Mike could see the look of fear on his face.

"Where are they? Are they here now?" Thomas said as he started looking around in a frantic way.

"No! They are gone for now, but I fear they will return soon. What is it they want?" asked Mike.

"They're some of Hobart's men. They have been trying to get me to tell them about your people!" O'Rourke said, almost in tears.

"Katelyn tried to warn me about how she thought someone had been following her around, and I would not listen."

"Who is Katelyn?" asked Mike.

"She is my niece and all that I have left in this world. Except my dear little ones!" Thomas said as tears roll down his cheeks. "I'm afraid I cannot take care of you any longer!" he said as he fell back on his pillows.

He was getting weaker by the moment. Holding out his hand to Mike, he muttered, "Must let Katelyn…know…how…to…find…little…ones. Help…them…leave…here!" And with that he closed his eyes and passed out.

Mike just sat there on the bed, wondering what he could do to help. But just then, at the back door, he heard, "O'Rourke! Open up! We want to talk to you!"

Thomas woke again and tried to answer them but had grown even weaker. He whispered to Mike, "Hide quickly!" He pointed to the door that led to the spare bedroom. "These are very bad men, and they mustn't find you here!"

Mike jumped down to the floor and ran into the spare room. Just as he got inside the door, he heard, "Open the door, old man. We told you we would be back!"

O'Rourke tried again to sit up, but he was much too weak and fell back into bed just as the back door was forced open.

Mike hid behind the spare bedroom door. Peeking through the crack between the door and the doorframe, he saw the back

door swing open with a loud crash as wood splinters from the doorframe flew all over the room. Two of the big men he saw in the car came into the house. They were dressed all in black and looked very menacing. When they reached Thomas's room, the bigger man went over to the bed.

"Get out of my house," demanded Thomas in a very weak voice.

The man grabbed hold of the front of Thomas's nightshirt and with only one hand, lifted him nearly off the bed. "We told you that if you didn't call Mr. Hobart and tell him what he wanted to know, we would be back!"

Thomas started to say something. "You will never…" His eyes got wide then slowly closed for the last time.

The other man, seeing what had just happened, yelled, "Now look what you've done! Hobart will have our hides for this!"

"Shut up, fool, I'm thinking!" the big man said as he let go of O'Rourke and turned around to leave the room. Then he snapped his fingers and said, "I've got it! We don't tell Hobart we talked to the old man. We just say he was dead when we came in. Yeah, that'll work! Now let's get out of here!"

They started to leave. "No, wait! We had better call Hobart and find out what to do next."

Mike could hear everything the two men were talking about. They knew it was going to make Hobart very angry when they called him, but they had to call.

Hobart was livid and told them to torch the place and get out. When they went to get the gas can in the SUV, it was empty. So they climbed in the car and went to find a gas station.

Mike heard the car drive away and waited a little while. Then, carefully, he came out of hiding, went to the front window, and looked out to see if they had really gone. Seeing that they had, he returned to the man that was their only hope of finding a safe place to live.

Mike saw a phone on the nightstand. Remembering what he saw through the window next door, he climbed up on the bedside table, lifted the receiver off the phone, and dialed 911.

"Nine-one-one operator, what is you emergency?"

Mike, not sure what to do, yelled as loud as he could, "Help!"

"Hello? Do you need help? I can hardly hear you? Hello?" But there was no answer.

Mike heard a car pull up outside. He jumped down from the nightstand, ran to look out of the window, and saw the bad men getting out of the car again. This time, one of them was holding a red can.

"Petrol!" Mike exclaimed as he ran and hid behind a chair that wasn't far from the back door, thinking that if they burned the house he had a chance to get out through the doggy door.

The bad guys had just got to the back door when they heard a police siren.

"Let's get outta here!" one of them half yelled as they ran and scrambled back into their car and drove off.

As it turned out, the police hadn't been very far away when the 911 operator called them and reported the strange call from Mr. O'Rourke's number. The officers went to the front door, and when no one answered, they tried it only to find it was locked. Going around to find another way in, they saw the broken side door. They entered and quickly searched the house. When they found Mr. O'Rourke, they checked and saw that he was not breathing. A call was placed for an ambulance, and the rest of the house was searched. Michael stayed hidden.

Mike watched as the medics arrived and tried to revive Mr. O'Rourke. Then they put him on a stretcher and took him away.

After all of them left with Mr. O'Rourke's body, Mike was in shock and trying to figure out what to do when a young woman drove up and came to the front door. She saw that there was police tape across it. She called out, "Uncle Thomas?" But there

GARY E. REAVIS, SR.

was no reply. She went around to the side door and saw that it is broken.

She heard a car pull up in front of the house and went around to see who it was. When she saw the policeman getting out of the car, she went over and asked, "What is going on? Where's my uncle?"

"Sorry, miss, but there's been a bit of trouble here. May I ask who you are?"

"I'm Katelyn O'Rourke, Mr. O'Rourke's niece."

"Well, miss, we responded to a 911 call, and upon arriving, we found the side door had been forced open. We entered the premises to find the resident in his bed, deceased. We searched the house but found no one. We had just pulled away when we saw your car stop here, so we came back."

Katelyn was crying as she asked, "What... Was he murdered? Who did this?"

"We don't really know, miss. Right now we suspect foul play. But we won't know if that is the cause of your uncle's death until we hear from the medical examiner."

"Is there anything I can do to help?" she asked.

"Would you mind having a look around the house to see what if anything has been taken?"

"I can do that," Katelyn answered and started into the house just as the officers got another call and had to leave.

As he got into the police car, he announced, "We will be back as soon as possible."

"I will stay here and wait for you," Katelyn replied, and she entered the house.

Mike, having again returned to hide in the spare bedroom, watched as she entered the bedroom of her uncle and saw the mess made by the medics who had tried to revive her uncle.

Sitting down in the chair next his bed, she started to cry.

"Uncle! Uncle, I tried to tell you I thought someone was following me. I was afraid they would find you and make you show

THE TELLING 153

them where the little ones are hiding. What am I to do now? You told me if anything happened to you I was to go to them and help them. But how can I find them? Why didn't you tell me? You were so afraid that I might be hurt if Hobart's men found out I knew about them. Now no one knows! How can I ever find them to warn them?"

Mike, after hearing this, stepped out from his hiding place and said, "I think maybe I can help!"

New Benefactor

Katelyn O'Rourke jumped with a start and turned to see this tiny man standing in the doorway of the spare bedroom.

"Sorry, miss!" said Michael, "I didn't mean to give you a start! But I do believe I can help you," he continued with a big grin on his face.

"I suppose you can indeed!" Katelyn replied while wiping the tears from her eyes. Taking a tissue from the bedside table, she dabbed at her eyes and nose, looked at him over the tissue, and asked, "Where in the world did you come from?"

"I'm afraid I have been here all along," he answered, shaking his head sadly. "It was some thugs that work for Hobart! They came in and tried to get Mr. O'Rourke to tell them where we were. I mean to say, where my people are."

"Did they see you? They didn't hurt you, did they?"

"No, miss, they didn't see me because your uncle told me to hide."

Sitting there, still sniffling and looking down at the tissue in her hand, she asked, "Did Uncle Thomas say anything else?"

Michael walked over to stand next to her. "He said he never had a chance to tell you how to contact us. I believe he thought you were in danger from those men."

Katelyn looked down at him and tried to smile. "Oh! I'm all right; he worried too much about me." Again the tears started to

fall, "I tried to warn him, you know. He was so weak, and I was afraid they would hurt him!"—*sniff*—"And now they have!"

Michael reached up and touched her hand, "It will be okay, miss. We'll help you!"

Now she smiled a little. "I thought I was supposed to help you!" She laughed.

Michael climbed up on the bed and sat down. "Well, I guess we'll just have to help each other!"

With a questioning look on her face, "I'm afraid I don't have any idea of where to start."

Just then there is a knock on the front door. "Police, open up please!"

"Hide quickly!" she whispered as she started for the door. Looking back over her shoulder, she saw Mike running back into the spare bedroom. When she got to the door, she looked through the peephole before opening it. She saw a policeman and a police car outside. So she opened up the door.

"Miss, did you find anything missing or out of place?" asked the policeman.

Katelyn indicated for him to come in and replied, "I'm sorry. I'm afraid I've been crying and haven't looked yet!"

"That's okay, miss. If I may, I would like to take a second and have a look for myself?"

"Oh, sure go ahead."

As they both walked back to her uncle's bedroom she asked, "What are we looking for?"

The officer took out a notebook and wrote in it as they walked. He looked up to say, "We think that whoever broke in must have wanted to rob your uncle. But they were stopped when he managed to place a nine-one-one call. We just happened to be in the area, and I'm sure our siren must have chased them away."

Katelyn, not wanting to give away any information, said, "Yes, that must have been it. Although, I can't imagine what they were after. My uncle never has had much in the way of money. The

only thing I recall he had that might be worth anything would be his collection of comic books and a few old hardback books he loved."

While they slowly worked their way through the house, Michael ran into the closet, quickly climbed up a coat, and got onto the top shelf. He scrambled over a stack of magazines and hid behind them.

"Do you know where he would have kept his collection?" asked the policeman as they entered the room where Michael was hiding.

Katelyn went over to the closet, opened the door, and pointed to the stack of comic books, not thinking Michael might hide there.

The officer looked at them and started to reach up then changed his mind. "Does it appear that they're all there?" he asked.

Katelyn took a long look. As she was checking the books, she noticed a tiny shoe sticking out from behind one of the stacks. She turned around quickly and replied, "Yep! As far as I can see, they are all there!"

The officer closed his notebook and turned to leave. "Okay then, I think we have covered everything for now. Of course you will need to come down to the station and file a report."

"Of course," Katelyn remarked. "I must call a repairman to fix the door, and then I'll be down."

"Good! Sorry for your loss, miss," he said with a tip of his hat and went out the door.

After she had made sure that the police had gone, she hurried back into the room where Mike was. "You can come out now; it's safe!"

Mike slowly climbed down the same coat he used before. As he landed on the floor, Katelyn said with a sigh, "I almost blew it with the comic books! I never dreamed you'd be up there."

Mike smiled up at her and said, "And I thought it looked like a very good place to hide!" He laughed. Then he turned very seri-

ous. "Katelyn, I must go back now and report what has happened. Will you be safe here?"

Katelyn kneeled down and took his tiny hand in hers. "I will be all right, but I have a question."

"What is it you wish to know?" answered Michael.

She grinned and asked, "What's your name, sir?"

Michael laughed out loud and said, "My apologies, miss! My name is Michael Flanagan!"

"Michael Flanagan, is it then, and a lovely name at that!" She giggled. Then she questioned, "How am I to contact you? And what are we to do about getting you to America? Or finding a safe place for you?"

He took off his tiny hat and scratched his head. "I don't know what to do about how or where we are to go. I will have a talk with the elders and Lord willing return here to this house one week from today!"

She snapped her finger as if she has just remembered something important. "I just remembered! Uncle told me a secret way you little ones can get into the house."

Michael asked, "And what might that be?"

"There is an old dog house out in the back yard. It has a secret door at the back of it. You must push on the left side of one of the boards in the back. It is really a door, and it will open. Once inside, Uncle told me you just follow the instructions you will find on the wall," Katelyn explained.

"I saw this dog house earlier when I was in the backyard. So you just follow the instructions, is it?" Mike recalled.

"Yes! And I will be here. You must come at night. I will be in the house with no lights on just in case the house is being watched by those Hobart men," reminded Katelyn.

"Just where does this secret passage open in the house? I would not like to walk into one of those bad men as I come in, you know!" Mike asked.

"Oh! Here, I can show you. It's under the kitchen sink," she said as she got up and headed for the kitchen. She went over to the sink and opened up the cabinet door. Getting down on her knees, she reached behind all the cans and bottles of cleaning stuff and showed him what looked like a place where the back wall was repaired with a panel of plywood.

"When you come in, you can stop under here. Listen to see if I am alone, or if those men are here before you come out from under the sink, okay?"

"Yes! That will work!" said Mike. "And now I must go!" And he headed for the broken back door. He stopped at the door and turned to ask, "What are you going to do about this?" He pointed to the door.

"I know a man that can replace it. I will call him now and have it fixed and made more secure."

Mike nodded his head, tipped his hat, and then turned to go. Before he reached the door, Katelyn heard him say, "The Lord keep you safe, Katelyn O'Rourke!"

She answered back, "And you as well, Michael Flanagan!"

Call for Help

It took Michael that night and the next day to reach the caves where the others were waiting.

He told Shawn Dugan and the elders all he had seen and heard at the O'Rourke house. They all said a prayer for their old benefactor they had grown to love then told Michael to go rest and they would let him know when they'd reached a decision.

By now Michael was tired to the bone, wanting nothing more than a meal and a few hours' sleep. Just as he rounded the corner in the cave where his makeshift house was, he saw a light coming from his doorway and he thought to himself, *Now what? Who can this be? I told them all I know...*

Just then Miss Drew Fitzpatrick poked her head out of the door and announced, "I was thinkin' you would be hungry. So I fixed your breakfast for you, Michael Dugan, and I'll have none of your sass about it!"

"Aye, and you'll get none from me, lass, and thank you!" Michael gave a tired reply.

"Oh! Lass, is it now? Well it wasn't lass when you kissed me good-bye a week ago!" she answered.

Michael sat down on the front step. "Now, Drew, you know it's the tiredness in me that's talking now! Don't get angry with me. I'm so tired I don't know what I'm saying, except I love..." And he passed out.

Drew almost dropped the skillet of food she was holding. She quickly put it on the fireplace, came out, sat down next to him, pulled his head up, and placed it on her lap. "Oh, Michael, I was

so worried about you. I almost lost my mind! I missed you so. Please be all right!"

Michael, without opening his eyes, in a low voice said, "'Tis true that I love you, lass!"

Drew hugged him and cried, "And I love you, Michael!"

It had been almost a week since Michael's return. When he was asked to meet with the elders again, Shawn made an announcement. "Mike, we have decided to send you back with the information Miss O'Rourke will require in order for her to contact the beneficiary in America. Now, we have never done this before. Not in my lifetime or in any of the others' before us. This address was given to me at my last meeting with Thomas O'Rourke. He was feeling sick and was concerned for us if something should happen to him. We now know something did! Do you feel up to another run back to town, Lad?"

"Yes, I'm okay now. I had a good rest and some very fine meals!" replied Mike.

They all laughed, knowing that the lass, Drew, finally declared her love for him and had taken good care of him.

"Well then, off with you. Above all, don't let that piece of paper fall into the wrong hands!"

The trek through the woods back to the O'Rourke house was uneventful. Mike made very good time, arriving again just as the sun was setting.

As he approached the neighborhood, he noticed that the O'Rourke house was dark. No lights could be seen in any of the windows. As he had done the last time he was here, he cautiously moved around to the front of the house.

Again he spotted the big black SUV parked just down the block. This time he couldn't tell if anyone was in it. He stayed in the underbrush, just waiting to see if anyone was either in the

house or nearby. He didn't hear or see anything, so he moved around back to try the secret way in through the dummy doghouse.

All this time Katelyn has been hiding inside the house. She had arrived there about two hours ago and had entered through the side door. When it started getting dark, she left the lights off so anyone looking at the place would think that no one was there.

But sitting in the dark waiting was becoming very spooky. About ready to give up and leave, she heard a noise coming from the kitchen.

She reached over and grabbed hold of the golf club she had found in her uncle's closet earlier. Standing up, she moved quietly to one side of the kitchen doorway. She brought the club up and was ready to strike whoever came through that door.

When Mike opened the secret door that let him into the house, he knocked over a can of cleanser that was under the kitchen sink. He waited a few moments before opening the cabinet door and coming out from under the sink. He stood there with the cabinet door open, ready to scamper back outside if anything was wrong. He had thought he had heard movement just as he opened the cabinet door, but it stopped.

Then a faint voice called from the front room, "Michael, is that you?" Katelyn said as she peeked around the door.

Seeing her face, he stepped clear of the cabinet door and answered, "Would you be thinkin' that there be pixies stumbling about in the dark? Would you now?" He laughed.

She came around the door and upon seeing him sat down on the floor and held out her hand for him to come to her. He ran over and jumped into her lap.

"I've been so frightened!" she said, pointing in the direction where the SUV was parked. "Those men arrived about an hour ago. They've been just sitting there, waiting."

"Aye! I saw the car as I took a wee look around before coming in. Do you know who they are or what they want?" he questioned as he looked up at her.

"Yes, yes, I do! Thanks to a lady who works for their boss, I know everything!" she replied.

"Are we safe here then?" asked Mike.

"Well, I don't believe they know I'm here. But they are dangerous and will stop at nothing to get their hands on you and your people!" Then she told Michael that this Hobart family had been trying to find his clan for generations. "Do you know what that is all about?" she inquired.

Mike knew all about the Hobarts. Right then he didn't want to be too free with any information. "I'm not sure. Do you think we need to leave and go someplace else?"

"I'm afraid they might see us leave. How can we get them to go away?" she asked.

Mike thought for a while and then asked, "Is the phone still working?"

"I believe so," she said, getting up, and she started to pick it up when she froze. "What if they bugged the phone?"

"Bugged?" asked Mike. "What do you mean, lass?"

"They could have put a device in it so that they can hear when someone makes a call," she explained.

"Well then that won't do, will it now!" Mike exclaimed.

"Wait!" she almost shouted. "I have my cell phone in my purse. We can use it!"

"And what of those men, won't they hear it too?" questioned Mike.

"No, no! I've had it with me all along, so they couldn't have put anything in it," she explained.

"Good, then call the police," Mike said.

"But they will ask questions," she argued.

"Simply tell them that you think these are the same men who broke in last week," Mike encouraged.

But before they could make the call, they heard a commotion outside. Both of them went over to the front window. Mike climbed up on a chair so he could see outside. Two cop cars had

pulled up to block the SUV. The police approached the SUV with guns drawn. Mike and Katelyn wondered what was going on.

It turned out that there was an anonymous caller who claimed to be out walking his dog when he noticed the black SUV parked near the O'Rourke house. The caller remembered that on the night of the attempted robbery and Mr. O'Rourke's death he saw this same SUV parked by the O'Rourke house.

Again, the police were only a few blocks away, but this time there were two units on the scene. They both responded quickly, approaching the SUV from two different directions and blocking them in.

While these dummies were supposed to be watching the O'Rourke house, the driver, Dick, was busy listening to the radio. Harry was in the back seat cleaning his gun, and Tom was asleep with the wiretap earphones on his head. When the police arrested them and searched the car, they found two cans of gas, burglary tools, and telephone bugging and recording equipment with all the tapes they had illegally recorded including their phone calls to Randal Hobart.

Back in the house, Mike and Katelyn watched as the three men were handcuffed and taken away.

"Well, now I wonder how that happened." Katelyn remarked. "I hope that takes care of those three for a while."

Michael was glad to see the danger had passed for now. Still worried about what they were going to do to solve his little group's problem, he said, "I'm glad to see them gone. I wonder just how long it will be before they or someone else like those thugs are back looking for us."

Katelyn turned away from the window and sat down on the floor next to this brave little man. "Did you bring the contact information? We must hurry and try to get help from America!"

"Yes, I have it right here," he answered as he pulled out the paper from inside his shirt.

"Tell them to bring one of the Tinys with them so that we can be sure who they are. Also, have the Tiny meet me here using the secret way into the house. Tell them to meet us one week from today. They must only bring one Big person with them. That way we can take every care not to be trapped or tricked."

"Yes, I'll tell them. I will be here as well, just as I was tonight," she announced.

Michael looked up at her and, seeing the deep concern on her face, said, "It will be all right now, Katelyn, lass. Don't you worry none!"

Then he thought to himself, *Now what will she be doing with herself when the likes of us are gone off to America, I wonder."* Then he asked her, "Katelyn, do you have family here?"

She looked down at a tiny, worried, tired face and replied, "No! I have no one now that Uncle is gone! Why do you ask?"

"Well, I was just wondering what you were going to do when we are gone."

"I don't know. I guess I will stay in London for now. There is the business to look after, you know."

"Why don't you think about coming with us to America? You are our benefactor now, you know!"

Tiny Commandos

At Hawk Industries headquarters in Nashville, Janet was busy in her office with the daily running of the company. Her secretary came in with a registered letter from Ireland. Janet immediately stopped what she was doing and opened it. After reading it, she told her secretary to cancel all her appointments for the rest of the day. The minute the secretary left Janet's office, she picked up the duplicate cell phone to the one she gave Conor and dialed his number. When he answered the phone she said, "Conor, this is Janet."

"Hi, Janet, what's up?"

"I need to meet with you, Grandpa, and the gentleman I met the last time I was at Grandpa's house."

"Okay. Is there a problem?"

Trying to disguise her message, she answered, "Just a little one, but I'm afraid it requires our immediate attention."

"Okay, do you want us to come there?" he asked.

"I don't think that'll be necessary. I can meet you halfway, if you think the gentleman can travel that far. Ask Grandpa if we can meet at the place where he and I met the last time," Janet said.

"Okay, just a minute," he said and turned to his grandfather. "I believe there is a problem, and Janet can't tell me over the phone. She wants to meet at the last place you two met."

"Oh," Grandpa said, and he sat up in his easy chair. "That's a code word for Big trouble and to be careful! Tell her that will be fine, and we'll be there at seven fifteen tonight."

Conor frowned and then gave her the message, and they both hung up. He looked at Grandpa and asked, "Seven fifteen p.m.? How did you come up with that time?"

"It's another code, Scooter, that tells her where we're really going to meet!"

"Oh! Huh?"

"I'll explain it in the car. Go get Graybeard, and tell him it's an emergency!"

After Conor went to the Tinys' village and got Graybeard, he, Graybeard, and Grandpa climbed into the new car that Conor just got, and off to Nashville they went. After a two-hour drive, they arrived at the Hawk Industries headquarters building just east of the Nashville airport. The main building covered a city block and stood twenty stories tall.

Grandpa told Conor to pull into the underground parking garage. Once they were inside, he told him to head to the southwest corner. Grandpa pointed toward a group of three freight elevator doors. As they got closer, Grandpa pulled a remote-control unit out of his pocket and pushed a button. The left door opened.

"Drive into that one there!"

"Drive in?" questioned Conor.

"Go ahead, it's okay," Grandpa said.

Once the car was completely inside the elevator, Grandpa pushed another button, and the door shut; then they started to descend. They dropped down a few floors before coming to a stop at sublevel five. When the door opened, Conor saw a well-lit tunnel that looked like it ran for at least a quarter of a mile. He drove into it, and Grandpa told him to turn at the second left. As he did he saw that it was a dead end with four parking spaces. He pulled in, parked, and turned off the engine and looked over at Grandpa.

"This is more like something you see in a spy movie than a corporation office. Why all this secrecy?"

As Grandpa and Graybeard were getting out of the car, Grandpa explained, "Well, we do a lot of work for the government and military. Some of our own projects are secret, and this is necessary in order to keep them secret!"

He and Graybeard started toward a door. Grandpa stopped and turned around to find Conor still standing by the car, looking around.

"What's wrong, Grandson?"

"Nothing. It's just so Hollywood-like and surreal!"

"Well, besides the need for secrecy, Scooter, I've always kind of liked those Double Oh Seven movies." Graybeard and he laughed.

Conor caught up with the two of them. They went through a door into an outer office. Ed Barns was waiting inside. He got up from behind the desk, came around, and greeted them.

"Good evening, Mr. O'Brien," he directed at Grandpa. Looking down at Graybeard, he asked, "And how are you tonight, Mr. O'Doul?" Then he looked up at Conor. "And how's the new boss?" as he held out his hand and shook Conor's.

"But, you're that driver from the airport, the one who drove Grandpa and me around?"

"Yes, sir, I'm Ed Barns, Mrs. Cook hired me as your, shall we say, assistant." Ed was a very confident fifty-seven-year-old ex-CIA agent that stood six-foot-two with a muscular frame and a handsome smile. Those piercing gray-blue eyes seemed to see everything, and his dark-brown hair he always wore short military style was just starting to gray around the temples. His dark-blue suit showed off his broad shoulders but concealed much. He discreetly opened his jacket to reveal a gun tucked neatly under his arm. "Welcome to your little home away from home!"

He turned and opened the door to the meeting room. After everyone was inside, Ed stepped in, closed the door, and remained

inside. The first thing Conor noticed was the lovely lady sitting on one of the couches placed off to the side of the room. Janet got up from the couch and came over to where they were all standing.

"Evening, guys," she said casually and indicated they should join her on the couches.

As they all sat down, she smiled at Conor. "Well, what do you think of your grandfather's hideout? Kind of James Bondish, isn't it?"

"I would say so!" Conor answered as he looked around with a worried look on his face.

Janet saw his concern and asked, "Something bothering you, Conor?"

"I was just wondering what else I might find in this Double Oh Seven land we call Hawk Industries," Conor remarked.

"I had planned to finish giving you the tour this week, but now we have this trouble in Ireland," she said, and she handed him the letter from Katelyn O'Rourke.

Everyone read the letter containing all the details about the Hobarts and their search for the Tinys, all of which Hobart's secretary gave to Katelyn.

Conor, who had been writing in his ever-present notebook, looked up. "What can we do to help them?"

Janet answered, "The way I see it, we need to do three things. First and foremost is to ensure the safety of the Tinys in Ireland! Second is to come up with a way to remove all evidence of the Tinys' existence from the hands of the Hobarts. And third, come up with a way to discredit the Hobarts."

Ed Barns, who had been taking all this in, spoke up, "Since the aunt has such a fascination about the Tinys, I think you should have her make their acquaintance in a Halloween kind-of way!"

"A what?" asked Janet with a surprised look on her face.

Ed laughed and answered, "I was thinking that with the help of the Tinys, we could scare the Tinys right out of her. In a way that would make her not want to see another Tiny, *ever*!"

Graybeard laughed. "Now that sounds like fun! Can I get in on that?"

"Me too!" chimed in Grandpa. "I can think of a few things the Tinys can do to her that will curl her hair!"

"Okay! Then you three put your heads together and come up with some ideas. Don't forget you have very little time, but all the resources of the company," Janet said.

Conor checked his notes and then asked Janet, "Miss O'Rourke's letter did say that Hobart's secretary was willing to help us in any way, did she not?"

Janet nodded her head yes.

"Good, that's what I thought. I was thinking it would be a good idea to arrange a meeting in London with Miss Baryl, Miss O'Rourke, Ed, you, and me as soon as possible," Conor detailed.

"That's a very good idea, Conor, but I'm not so sure you should be involved in this." Janet commented.

"Well, I have to start being involved sometime. What do you think, Grandpa?"

"He's right; you might as well take him with you." Grandpa said, "And besides, I want Conor to start coordinating anything that has to do with the Tinys."

"Okay, I'll get right on it," Janet replied.

"I think we should bring Scott Curtis, my dad's friend from Micro Technology. He is a brilliant engineer, and I know my dad trusted him completely. I think he would be a big help if we invite him into our little circle of tiny friends. I need some things built for the Tinys, and he is just the man to get it done and quietly. So does anyone have a problem with me letting him in on our secret?" Conor asked. Conor looked from face to face, and they all shook their heads no.

"Okay! Janet, can you have him fly in tomorrow? I'll go over what I want from him before we leave for London."

"Sure, I will call him when we are finished," Janet replied.

Ed asked Janet, "Correct me if I'm wrong, didn't we see our new, long-range corporate jet prototype over at Hawk Aviation getting ready to go through its final long distance flight tests?"

"Why, yes we did," Janet confirmed.

"Good! Then that's how we will transport the Irish Tinys back here to Tennessee."

Janet, a bit puzzled, questioned, "How can we pull that off? With all the heightened security and going through customs in both the US and Ireland, it will be impossible!"

Ed answered, "I noticed that the test plane was jammed full of test gear and equipment. We will simply replace some of it with dummy equipment. That way we'll have room to build little seats for our small friends. We will of course have to come up with a plan on how we will get them from where they are now to the airport in Dublin."

"Any ideas?" When no one said anything, he took a deep breath and decided it was time for him to put his expertise to use, turned to Graybeard. "Okay! I need you to pick four or five Tinys to come with us to Ireland who will work with the Irish scouts or whatever they call themselves. Once we arrive, there are two important tasks they'll be needed for.

"First, they will need to make contact with the Irish Tinys as per the instructions in the letter. Second, they will be to infiltrate both the home of Hobart's Aunt and Hobart's office. Can you do that?"

Graybeard scratched his beard and said, "Yes, I think I have just the scouts we'll need for the job. But I do have one question?"

"What is it?" Ed asked.

"Well, don't you think that the Hobart building and offices will be highly secured?"

"You're right about that, but I think if our meeting with Miss Baryl goes as I suspect, we'll have no problem with access," Ed explained.

"Oh, yes, that would be a great help. I forgot for a moment that she is willing to help us," Graybeard acknowledged.

Ed leaned back in his chair, and announced, "If there are no more questions, I suggest we all get to work on getting the Tinys out of Ireland and home here to Tennessee!"

Conor announced, "I think we should call this *Operation Rainbow*."

"Very good idea, Conor!" Janet exclaimed. "*Operation Rainbow* it is!"

The next day in Ireland, Katelyn O'Rourke got an overnight registered letter from Janet. It read:

To: Katelyn O'Rourke

Dublin, Ireland

Miss O'Rourke, we received your letter and understand that you have a small problem that requires our attention.

Per your instructions, we have put things in motion here, and the interested parties should arrive there at the appointed date and time.

We understand that the item mentioned will need to be moved to another location, and we are making preparations to do so.

We have heard that a third party is also interested in the item, and we are going to make them a separate offer.

Should the matter require immediate attention, please go to the Hawk building in Dublin at 446 Main Street and see Mr. John Harold. He will have further instruction and a secure phone for you to use to get in touch with me.

Sincerely
Janet Cook
CEO Hawk Industries.

Janet also sent an overnight registered letter to Heather Baryl. It read:

To: Heather Baryl

London, England

Miss Baryl, your name has reached my desk in our search for quality personnel.

I believe we have a friend in common. We are aware of the assistance you gave to her with her little problem.

We would like to meet with you to discuss a similar problem we have here in the US.

We also understand that you will be retiring from you present position soon. We feel that you would be a valuable member of our team.

To that end, we would like to extend to you an offer for a position as a consultant. Please reply.

Sincerely,
Janet Cook
CEO Hawk Industries.

That night Heather called Katelyn. "Katelyn, this is Heather."
"Hi, Heather!"
"Did you get a letter today?"
"Why, yes I did! Did you?"
"Yes, and I don't know what to make of it. Can we meet and talk it over?"
"I'm still in Ireland, but I'll take the next plane and be in London around two p.m.
"Let's meet at the same spot at three p.m.," Katelyn said, and she hung up.

That afternoon they met in the park. Heather seemed a bit nervous and told Katelyn, "I am very worried that Mr. Hobart might find out about my talking to you. Now I got an offer from a company in America! I really don't know what to make of this." She handed the letter to Katelyn.

Kate read it, and when she saw the signature at the bottom, she smiled and said, "This is from the people in America that are going to help my little ones. So it appears that they want you to come to America and work for them. I think it is a kind of reward for your helping me!"

Heather laughed. "You mean I don't have to worry anymore about losing my job?"

Katelyn gave her a hug. "That's the way I see it!"

Then Heather broke down and cried.

The next morning:

Scott arrived in Nashville after a twenty-minute limo ride from the airport to Hawk Industries headquarters. Janet's secretary took him to one of the unoccupied offices, where he found young Conor busy working at a modeling computer.

Conor looked up as Scott came in. "Hi, Scott, how was your flight?"

"Okay! Kind of early at four thirty a.m., but other than that, just ducky!" Scott joked.

"Yeah! Sorry for the short notice and the early hour, but we have a special problem, a very tight schedule, and a lot that needs to be done," Conor said.

Scott set down his briefcase and coat then walked over to the computer. "Okay! What's up?"

"First I need to ask you a question," Conor led out.

"Okay, shoot. What's on your mind?" Scott inquired.

Conor tried to hold back a grin. "Do you believe in little people?"

"Huh? Little people? You mean like dwarfs and the like?"

"No, more like leprechauns and fairies."

"Leprechauns? No, I don't believe in fairy tales! Why do you ask?" Scott questioned.

Just then Janet walked in. "Hi, Scott!" she said and smiled.

He returned her smile and said, "Hi, Janet, nice to see you again."

Scott and Janet had met before at one of the company functions. They both liked each other right from the start. Afterwards when Scott asked a few of his friends about her, he learned that she had been a widow for five years and had a teenaged daughter.

"You too," she said. Now she was grinning from ear to ear!

He got a funny feeling and looked back and forth between the two smiling faces. "Hey, what's going on here? What's this all about?"

Janet, who was still standing in the doorway, moved a little to her right, and out from behind her pant leg stepped Graybeard.

Scott looked from Janet to Graybeard, to Conor, to Graybeard, to Janet, back to Graybeard, and back to Janet, and finally at Graybeard.

"*Wow!*" was all he could muster up to say.

Graybeard walked right up to him and held out his hand. "Glad to meet you, Scott. I've heard very good things about you."

Scott looked like he was going to faint. "*Wow!* I can't believe… How in the…Where did…*Wow!*"

"Sounds just about like what I said when I first meet him," Conor said.

They all laughed.

Janet walked over and took Scott's hand and pulled it down to meet Graybeard's. Taking Scott's thumb and finger, she closed it on Graybeard's hand and shook it.

"See, he won't *bite*!" She laughed. "Oh! By the way, he's *not* a leprechaun or a fairy for that matter!"

"Oh! That's good to know!" Scott managed to get out.

Janet led him over to the couch and sat down with him. He was still staring at Graybeard when Conor started telling him all about the Tinys and how he and his family, and now a few friends, became the Tinys' protectors and benefactors. He continued to tell him all about their history, the trouble that Hobart and his Aunt were causing the Irish Tinys, and what Conor and his little group planned to do about it.

He was explaining all this to Scott when he noticed that Janet was still holding Scott's hand. He grinned and kept on with the where, what, and who of their plan to rescue the Tinys in Ireland.

After he finished he asked, "Do you have any questions?"

Scott said, "I don't know where to start. You really think you can just go over there and take on Hobart and his tough guys and pick up how many tiny people? And then bring them back here, and *nobody* is going to say or do anything?"

Graybeard asked, "Conor, may I say something?"

"Of course, go right ahead."

"Scott, I'm glad you see the difficulties that we must overcome. This is one of the reasons Conor wanted you on the team. We have come up with a plan that we think will work. But I would like for you to go over it with Conor and Janet, just to see if you can find anything that might cause our plan to fail. Isn't that what you both want?" he asked, indicating Janet and Conor.

"Yes, of course!" Janet said.

Conor agreed, "Yes, that's what I want, and when you finish, I have some designs for things we will need to take with us. I would like it if you to look them over and if you approve, get the shops working on them right away! We leave for Ireland a week from tomorrow."

Scott shook his head. "Go to Ireland. Beat up bad guys. Break into a man's office and steal documents. Rescue little people. Smuggle them out of Ireland and into the US; should be a piece of cake!"

There was silence for a moment, and then Janet said, "Lord, help us!"

And everyone said, "Amen!"

New Revelations

The next morning, Scott called Conor on the secure phone he was given. "Conor, I need to talk to a few of the little people and get some idea of what they can do physically and mentally. Can you arrange it?"

"I can do better than that. I'm tied up over here working on the jet with Ed, but I'm sure Janet won't mind taking you to my grandpa's house," Conor replied.

"Grandpa's house?" questioned Scott.

"You will understand better once you get there," Conor said.

"Okay! You're the boss!" Scott remarked.

"Ah, cut it out, Scott. You know I'm not the boss, yet!" Conor joked.

"Oh! By the way, they liked to be addressed as Tinys, not little people," Conor added.

"Tinys," Scott answered. "Okay! Got it. Oh, and you did say you were going to ask Janet to take me, right?"

"You kind of like her, don't you?" teased Conor.

"That I do, Conor, that I do!" Scott exclaimed.

"Good, I'll give her a call and then set up a meeting with the Tinys," Conor said. "I'll have to get back to school tomorrow."

"Okay! See you later, and Conor."

"Yeah?"

"Thanks for the new job, boss."

"Will you stop that?" Conor said, and they both laugh.

It was about five minutes later when Janet walked into Scott's new office. Of course it was only two doors down from hers.

"Good morning, Scott."

"Good morning. Did Conor call you just now?" Scott asked as he got up from his desk and came around to greet her.

"Yes, he did, and I would be glad to take you to Grandpa's house. I have called the airport, and the helicopter will be here in thirty minutes. I assumed you were in a hurry," Janet remarked, "so I cleared my calendar for the day."

"Thank you! I'm glad you can show me around. I'm still trying to catch up on all of this. I can use all the help I can get," Scott commented.

They talked for a few minutes. Then it was time to go up to the roof to catch the helicopter. As they come out the door to the helicopter pad, Scott saw Ed Barns waiting by the chopper. "Good morning, Mrs. Cook, Mr. Curtis," Ed said, and after seeing the puzzled look on their faces he added, "Conor asked me to be in on this little adventure."

"Good!" Janet exclaimed. "Let's go!"

They all climbed in and took off for Jamestown. After they had their headsets on, Janet said, "I called Grandpa, and he's arranged for us to meet them at his house. I have a rental car waiting at the airport." Then she turned to Scott. "Is there anything else you need?"

"Yeah, can you hold my hand? I'm afraid of flying!" Scott exclaimed. Janet quickly took his hand and held it tight. She didn't notice the smile on Ed's face; he turned away to look out the window in time to hide it. He knew from doing the background checks that Scott was a licensed pilot and had hundreds of hours logged in the air. He thought to himself, *Nice move, buddy!*

Once they arrived at Grandpa's house, Scott and Ed were introduced to a few of the Tinys Grandpa and Graybeard thought could help with Operation Rainbow.

Graybeard cleared his throat and announced, "Let me introduce everyone. Our little group consists of Gary, our blacksmith and handy man that can make just about anything out of very little. Vaughn is our teacher and the keeper of knowledge. You might call him a historian. Our best scouts, Eric and his brother Bryan. And then there's me. Now, what can we do for you?"

"Well, I need to test all of you to determine what you can do physically and mentally. That is, if you don't mind?" Scott explained.

"What are these tests for?" questioned Vaughn.

"Are you all familiar with Operation Rainbow?" Scott asked.

Graybeard spoke up, "Yes, they have all been briefed."

"Good! What I need to do is to construct some gadgets for the team of Tinys that are going to Ireland, but in order to make things that will help and not hurt you, I need to know your limitations."

The Tinys all looked at one another, and Graybeard nodded his head to give the okay.

Now Gary stepped forward and said, "I have a few ideas and drawings that might help."

Vaughn spoke next. "Scott, we know this is all new to you, so maybe I can help out. First, every Tiny, when their IQ is tested, tests above average. There are a few of us that score much higher. And some of us, like Eric and Bryan, also have above average physical abilities."

"What kind of physical abilities?" asked Scott.

Again the Tinys looked to Graybeard for the okay, and he nodded yes again. Vaughn turned to Eric. "Show him."

Eric walked over to one side of the room, took out his knife, then tossed it up in an ark almost to the ceiling and across the room. Everyone's eyes were on the knife as it flew through the

air. When it reached the other side of the room, Eric was there to catch it.

Scott just stood there for a moment. Then he exclaimed, "That was amazing! Can all of you move that fast?"

"No, only a few are born with that gift. Some can communicate with birds and animals. Others have the knowledge to heal," Eric answered.

Scott was grinning from ear to ear while writing notes in his ledger. "Anything else?" he asked.

Gary walked over to Bryan and asked him to turn around so that Scott could see his backpack. When he did, the first thing Scott noticed was that he had it on upside-down. Then Gary took a red rock from his pocket and put it in Bryan's pack, leaving it open upside-down. All the others came over and took a red rock out of their pockets and placed them in Bryans backpack. All the while Scott was wondering what is going on. After everyone has placed a red rock in Bryan's pack, Scott noticed that Bryan was now hovering about six inches off the ground. Gary closed the backpack, and then he gently gave Bryan a shove that sent him sailing across the room floating in the air!

Scott came over to where Bryan was still floating and asked, "May I?" Bryan grinned.

"Sure, go ahead." Scott gave him a slight push, and off he went across the room again.

"How does that work?" Scott asked.

Graybeard spoke up this time. "These stones were found many years ago in a cave in England. A few of them came with us when we were brought here in 1919. They possess this lifting property, and we have learned how to use it, as you can see."

Gary remarked, "As you can imagine, they are not easy to work with. If you drop one, it will simply fly up and away!"

Scott was shaking his head. "I have never seen or heard of anything like this!"

Vaughn said, "I hope we have demonstrated what we can do to your satisfaction."

"You have done that and more. Is there anything else I should know?" Scott asked.

Bryan replied, "Well, I can show you how high we can jump, if that will help?"

"That would help a lot, go ahead."

So Bryan and the others all headed for the door.

"Wait! Where are you going? I thought you were going to show me how high you can jump?" Scott said.

As they started out the door, Bryan called back over his shoulder, "We have to go outside to show you."

So Scott picked up his laptop he had been making notes on and followed them outside to the front of Grandpa's house. Once everyone was out, Eric and Gary helped Bryan take off his backpack and tie it to the porch railing so it wouldn't fly away. Then Bryan went over to one side of the porch and bent down. Scott blinked, and just that fast, Bryan jumped up landing on the edge of the roof.

Scott was dumbfounded. "I can't believe my own eyes. You just jumped ten feet in the air in the blink of an eye!" He shouted as Bryan jumped just as quickly back to the ground with the same ease.

Vaughn commented, "He is one of our best jumpers, and a bit of a showoff at times!"

Bryan walked up to Scott, took out two red rocks from his pockets, then winked, and they all laugh. "So you tricked me!" Scott commented. Bryan patted his pockets to show Scott that he didn't have any more rocks in them.

"Stand still," he said, and he jumped up and landed on Scott's shoulder. Then he jumped up again did a flip over Scott's head and landed on the other shoulder. Bryan then jumped back down to the ground, landed, spun around once, and took a bow. "Ta da!"

Scott was writing furiously in his notebook and mumbling to himself, "Amazing, simply amazing!"

As everyone went back inside the house, Grandpa announced, "Let's all go into the dining room where Grandma and Janet have some lunch ready."

Gary, who was seated near Scott, was very interested in what things and projects he was working on. So he asked, "Scott, I was wondering if I might get to see your lab and learn more about what you are working on."

Scott swallowed the last bite of his ham sandwich, looked down at this little man sitting there on the table, and thought to himself, *I would love to have him in my lab so I could find out just how intelligent they really are!* Then he exclaimed, "I would like that very much! Janet, can we arrange for Gary and anyone else who wants to get access to my lab?"

Before Janet could answer him, Vaughn spoke up, "I would like to see your lab also!"

"Yes! We have a safe place for them to stay right in Hawk Headquarters," Grandpa said, looking up from his stack of pancakes. "We added a few rooms and things that are not on the recorded blue prints."

"Is it close to the lab?" asked Scott

"Yes!" Grandpa answered with a smile. "We put in an apartment complex; a network of passageways; shops, labs, and some supply rooms. All constructed in between the floors, right under our offices and labs. They have access to all the floors by way of tunnels, stairs, and the cutest little elevators made right inside the walls."

Scott just shook his head. "The more I learn about this operation around here, the less I think I know!"

And they all laughed.

"But wait!" Scott exclaimed suddenly. "How will they travel from here to there without taking the chance of being seen?"

Vaughn replied, "Let's go into Grandpa's den. I think Gary and I just might have a few ideas." So off go the three of them. Once there, Vaughn continued, "Gary and a few others have been watching NASCAR on TV with Grandpa, and I believe Gary has come up with something. Gary, you tell him."

Gary said, "I will be glad to, but it would be much easier to just show him my designs on Grandpa's laptop!"

"Laptop!" Scott exclaimed. "I didn't know Grandpa had a computer."

"Oh, he does. Conor got it for him, but Grandpa mostly plays games on it," Vaughn commented.

"But Conor showed us how to us it, and of course Gary found a drawing program he likes. He's been up here using it as much as he can," Vaughn remarked. "I find the Internet to be a very good way to do research."

Scott said, "I'm still finding it hard to understand how you Tinys are able to get along so well in our big world. I mean, you all adapt so quickly to so many different situations."

Vaughn asked, "Scott, did you know that back in the sixteen hundreds we thought we were the normal people? That you all were giants and that there were only a few of you?"

"Wow! When did your people find out that they were the exception?" Scott questioned.

"Around sixteen fifty when Count William Hawks, of England, discovered them living in the woods in northern England. He was the one who brought them out into the real world," Vaughn continued.

"I wonder how I would feel if I suddenly found out I was among a very small minority, and the rest of the world was inhabited by giants." Scott said.

Gary interrupted, "Scott, I have some plans drawn up on the computer; would you like to see them?"

"Yes, very much. What are you working on?"

THE TELLING

"Now, don't laugh, but I have been watching NASCAR on TV with Grandpa."

Now Scott interrupted, "Yes, I know; Vaughn told me."

Gary gave Vaughn a look and continued, "Anyway, I came up with an idea for a safety seat that one of us could ride in while being carried by a Big. It is designed like the ones being used in the race cars. Here, take a look." And he brought up the design on the computer screen.

Scott studied it for a while and then said, "That's a good idea, and I like the design, Gary. It will protect you if the container you're in is dropped." Then you could see the light of inspiration come on. "Hey! I think you have helped solve our first problem!" Scott exclaimed.

"How is that?" asked Gary.

"Well, I have to figure out how to infiltrate Hobart's office without being detected, and now that I have seen this seat design, here's what I think we can do…"

Working together over the next few hours, the three men, two Tinys, and one Big became not only friends but also colleagues.

Nightmare in Hobart Mansion

It all started when Graybeard came over to Eric's house and asked him and Bryan if they would be willing to help rescue the Tinys in Ireland. They both, of course, said yes even before they found out all the details. Graybeard explained to them the plan that Conor, Janet, Scott, Ed, and he had come up with and how it was to be made up of three parts.

First Janet was to locate a place in Ireland where the team could load the Tinys onto the Hawk 500 jet. She had come through with flying colors, finding an empty hanger for lease with living quarters right on the second floor. It was located on a private airstrip only a few miles from the O'Rourke house just outside of Dublin.

Second, Ed, with Conor tagging along and the two US Tinys were to fly the jet to Ireland. After they got through customs, they would hop over, land at the airstrip, and park it in the rented hanger.

From there they would drive the rental van, Janet had arranged, to near the O'Rourke house. Then Eric and Bryan would make contact with the Irish Tiny named Michael.

That being done, they would have Michael arrange for all the Tinys to go to a location where Conor could meet them with the van and transport them to the hanger.

Third Eric and Michael would form teams to take on Randle Hobart and his aunt. They would travel to England and there divide into two groups: one to take on the aunt and the other to hit Hobart's office with the help of his secretary, Miss Baryl.

Under a cloudy sky with no moon, the night was pitch black. A slight drizzle fell on Eric and his team of Tinys waiting in the woods for the night to come. Finally, he got the signal from Bryan who was sent ahead to make sure the coast was clear. A tiny pin of light came from under the bushes near the back of the Hobart mansion, the all clear!

Eric spoke into his mic, "Okay! Move out, and take your positions."

It had not taken him as long as he had thought it would to put together this team that was made up of Tinys from both the American and Irish groups. He had quickly found the men he needed to do the job. After only one day of rehearsals, he was confident they could pull this off with no problems. Now of course was the moment they had been waiting for…revenge!

Scott, Gary, Vaughn, and Conor had provided them with all the tools they needed to do the job. That included complete blueprints of the mansion and all its secret passageways. Thanks in part to Miss Baryl and an angry building contractor, who the Hobarts had refused to pay for all of his work on the place, saying his work was not up to specs and that he used cheap materials. The fact that he had been in business for fifteen years and was known for his quality work did not count and his case could not hold up under the pressure brought on by the Hobarts' high-priced lawyers. The courts ruled in the Hobarts' favor. How Ed found out about this guy and where to find him still baffled Conor and Scott.

Conor had learned that because of their size/weight ratio, the Tinys could jump much higher than someone would think. Whereas a normal man in very good condition could jump maybe five feet high or close to his own height, some Tinys can easily jump ten times his or her height.

Here is a list of some of the things Scott and Gary assembled that they could carry in their backpacks:

1. A spool of nylon thread, a winch, and AA batteries. Using a bow and arrow, a Tiny could shoot a line from the floor clear into the ceiling of a Big's house and wench himself up to the ceiling or across a room.
2. A bottle of superglue and a spray gun.
3. A container that could be filled with spray paint or knock-out spray.
4. Small, marble-sized balls that when thrown on the ground, break and fill the area with a very dense smoke.
5. Two tubes filled with ball bearings.
6. Two containers filled with chemicals and a spray gun. When the two were combined and sprayed out together, they made a spider-web like effect.
7. Special arrows that contained knockout medication. When the arrow hit a Big, the knockout stuff went into the skin but the arrow dropped out. It took three hits to put a full-sized man out!
8. Next they dressed up a few dozen G.I. Joe, twelve-inch action figures to look like the Tinys to be used as decoys.

Now it was up to the team to get inside the mansion and scare the heck out of Hobart's aunt!

Using GPS and the diagram of the estate, it was child's play to circumvent the security system and enter the house through a secret door and tunnel that ran under the garden. Once inside,

they split up into three groups; one went straight to the aunt's bedroom. Another hurried to make sure the servants were asleep and wouldn't see them. The third made their way to the security room to make sure there wasn't any evidence of them being there that night.

Inside the bedroom, they found it to be laid out just as the contractor had described it to them. A very large four-poster bed with a canopy dominated the area by sitting right in the center of the room, not touching any walls.

The contractor had told them that the aunt had a phobia about crawly things and bugs. Boy, were they going to us that against her. On the far wall was an ornate dressing table. In the corner was a lounge chair. In the opposite corner was a writing desk and chair. On the remaining wall was a larger dresser with a huge mirror on the back. Everything was exactly as he had told them. Now they went to work. Oh, and of course the aunt was fast asleep in her bed.

A loud cry for help woke her with a start. She opened her eyes and looked around to see who made that noise. She started to sit up in bed, but for some reason she couldn't move. Her arms felt like they were tied down, and now she felt something jumping on the foot of her bed. She raised her head enough to look down by her feet. She saw him! But it couldn't be… A leprechaun dressed all in green with his little hat and a red beard was jumping up and down on her bed.

Matilda passed out.

Sometime later, she woke up, slowly opened her eyes, and looked down again, but no one was there. She sat up and shook her head.

"I must have been dreaming," she said, and she lay back down and started to go back to sleep when all of a sudden her eyes

popped open, she sat up again, looked at the upper-right corner of the canopy, and saw a giant spider web and a big hairy spider!

She screamed, jumped out of bed, and ran to the door. *Bam!* She hit the wall. Wall? Where was the door? There should be a door here! She was now very confused, and to make things worse, when she looked back at the bed, the spider moved. She screamed again. She tried to find the light switch by the door, but the door was gone; where was the door?

Just then she saw him just standing there on her dresser.... .a leprechaun!

Matilda was shaking so bad she could hardly speak, but she asked, "What do you want?"

He slowly raised his arm and pointed his finger at her, and in a ghostly voice said, "You are the one who wanted to see us! You want to have us as your pets! You and your nephew are the ones who have been trying to find us! *Now you have!*" And, *poof*, he disappeared.

She fainted on the floor.

This time she woke up to music. A soft little tune was coming from somewhere in her room. She opened her eyes and sat up to find that she was back in bed. Remembering the spider, she quickly looked to her right. No spider and no web. Where was that music coming from?

Getting out of bed, she slipped on her robe, put her feet into her slippers, grabbed her cane, stood, and went to take a step, but she couldn't move her feet.

What's wrong with my legs? she thought. *I can't even lift my foot.*

Sitting back down on the bed, trying to lift her legs up, they wouldn't move. She strained and strained to lift her legs. All of a sudden, her feet popped out of her slippers that had been glued to the floor. The momentum sent her falling back on the bed to land on her back. Now she was looking up right at a leprechaun sitting suspended in midair, playing a flute!

She yelled and rolled out of bed. Still thinking she couldn't walk, she crawled over to where the door should be, but it wasn't there.

The Tinys had moved all the furniture around so that now the door was on the other side of the room.

While she was sitting on the floor trying to figure out what had happened to the door and how she could get away from these things, in the dim light she noticed one of them sitting on her dresser. Then she spotted another over on her desk.

No wait! There were three more of them! She saw another standing in the doorway to her closet. Now there was one on her bed jumping up and down! She was going out of her mind! She saw them everywhere she looked!

"Why are you here?"

"Your family has hunted us for hundreds of years. Now it's our turn to *hunt* you!"

"No, no! Go away! I don't want to see you anymore."

"But don't you want to play?"

"No! No. Have mercy on an old woman," Matilda cried.

"Mercy? You and your family have never shown mercy to anyone. Now you must pay! *You must pay!*"

"*No!*" she cried and fainted again.

Quickly they put everything back the way it was and left the mean and wicked old lady lying on the floor, and they disappeared into the night.

That was exactly where her maid found her the next morning. She was sobbing and blubbering about spiders and leprechauns, how they were after her and out to get her.

The servant called her nephew and told him that it looked as if she has gone completely mad. By the time he arrived with a doctor, she was comatose and had to be put in a sanitarium. They searched her room, but everything looked just like it always did. There were no signs that anyone or anything had been there the night before.

The Deal

Conor brought the nose of the Hawk 500 jet around to line up with the centerline of the runway and then announced, "Nashville tower, Hawk jet HJ four nine six on final for thirty-six."

"Copy, four nine six, clear to land!" was the reply from the tower.

Conor had had his private pilot's license for a year now, logging about three hundred hours of flying time. Most of his training had been with his dad, two years ago. But this was his first jet, and he really liked it. The Hawk 500 was a dream to fly.

Ed Barn sat in the pilot's seat. As he watched Conor sitting there in the co-pilot's seat, he was very pleased with this young man's flying skills.

As the wheels touched down and the jet slowed, Conor turned off the runway and stopped short of the taxiway.

"Nashville Ground, four ninety-six taxi to hanger."

"Four ninety-six, you're clear to taxi"

"Four ninety-six" was all Conor said as he advanced the throttles and taxis across the field to the Hawk Industries hanger. Waiting there for him was Scott and Janet. The plane came to a stop in front of the hanger, and the engines were shut down. The door just behind the wing opened to reveal Conor smiling from ear to ear,

"Ta da!" he said as he stepped down and came over to greet them.

"Well, I don't know how, but I got checked out in this baby in three days!"

"Does that mean that you can fly this thing all by yourself?" Scott asked as he pointed at the jet.

"No, I'm not old enough to fly a jet all by myself, so Ed will be the pilot in command, but I can fly her from the left seat, right Ed? "

"Yes, you can, Conor, so now we can start *Operation Rainbow*."

Later in London…

It had been two days since Randle Hobart had put his aunt into the sanitarium. He was on cloud nine. Everything was going his way. With her out of the picture, he had gained full control of Hobart Inc. and was making plans.

The search for the little ones and the treasure was not going well. Three of his operatives had been arrested in Ireland. But right now, he had other fish to fry. He was at his desk, looking over some proposals, when his secretary Miss Baryl buzzed him.

"Sir, a Ms. Cook is here to see you," she said through the intercom.

He looked up from his work, frowned, and pushed a button on his desk. "Ms. Cook? I don't recall an appointment with a Ms. Cook? What does she want?"

"She is here from America with a proposal from Hawk Industries," Ms. Baryl answered, and she smiled at Janet.

"A proposal, from Hawk? Send her in."

Miss Baryl opened the door to his office and escorted Janet to a chair in front of Hobart's massive, three-legged desk. Hobart didn't even rise to greet her or come around to shake her hand.

"So what sort of proposal do you have for me?" he asked.

Janet set down her new, specially built briefcase, sat back in the chair, and replied, "We are interested in purchasing all of Hobart Industries holdings in both America and Ireland."

Hobart almost fell out of his chair. He stood up. "You what?" he shouted.

Janet calmly picked up the briefcase and placed it on her lap. Opening it so that he couldn't see what was inside, she took out a very thick package of legal papers and placed them on his desk.

She had purposely put together a very large amount of legal jargon, knowing he was the type that would be too lazy to read everything.

"I think you will find our offer to be to your liking!" she said. After carefully closing and locking her briefcase, she gently placed it on the floor next to her chair, and she got up to leave.

She was halfway to the door when he looked up from starting to read the proposal and said, "Wait! What do you want from me?"

She smiled and said, "Simply to accept it! I will be in touch tomorrow, and by the way, this offer goes away at midday tomorrow!" And she left.

He sat down and just stared at the big stack of papers. He opened it up and started to read through all the "party of the first parts," etc. After about one minute, he just thumbed through most of it. When he got to the last page, where all the numbers appeared, he read the bottom line, whistled, and exclaimed out loud, "I'm rich! With Aunty out of the picture for now, I can pull this off. I'll take my share of this deal and forget all about this lousy business and go have some fun! By the time Aunty comes back around, if she ever does, it will be too late! Ha, ha, ha, ha!"

While all this was going on, inside the briefcase that Janet "forgot" was Michael and Eric. The two Tinys were sitting in their protective seats, listening to everything. They were wearing tight-fitting, black, one-piece jumpsuits and what looked like fighter pilot helmets.

Scott had used Gary's design and constructed their seats to be like those used by NASCAR. But of course, they were a bit smaller. The seats held them in tight and protected them in case they were dropped or knocked over. Using Conor's and his ideas, Scott put together this one-of-a-kind briefcase. Although it

looked like a regular briefcase, this high-tech device was built for just this one job: to get them into Hobart's office.

The occupants, who were snug inside, could see through the one-way siding and hear everything that was said in the office.

Earlier when Janet was waiting in Hobart's outer office, Miss Baryl had passed her the key. She had removed it from Hobart's desk earlier that day. Janet then slipped it into the briefcase. Now all the two Tiny men had to do was wait for Hobart to leave his office.

Hobart finally got up from his desk and came around it to leave. When he spotted the briefcase, he started to reach down to pick it up. Both Tinys froze, holding their breath as the shadow of the huge hand fell over them. Then he stopped…looked at it for a second, then shrugged and just left it there and walked over to his private elevator and left.

After the elevator door closed, Michael looked at Eric who was looking at him, and they both silently mouthed, "Whew!"

Once Hobart got in his car, he punched in his office number on his dashboard computer screen. When Ms. Baryl answered, he said, "I have left for the day. When that Ms. Cook calls tomorrow, tell her she has a deal! Oh, and tell her she left her briefcase in my office." The line went dead with a click.

If he could only have seen the smile on Heather Baryl's face.

She opened Hobart's office door, reached around, turned off the lights, and closed the door, leaving our two hidden Tinys in the dark.

Eric was the first to act. He flipped open the cover on his arm-mounted computer to see the keyboard. With the cover open, he could see the display screen, which was mounted inside the cover. The screen came on, and he silently typed, "How long do you think we should wait?"

Michael, who was seated in front of Eric, felt his device vibrate. He reached over, opened it, and read Eric's message. Then he

replied, using his keyboard, "I should think another hour would do it!"

Not wanting to have their voices picked up by any hidden microphones, the two had pre-arranged this silent mode of communication before they got into their hideaway briefcase. Even though Heather had assured everyone that the office was clean, with the exception of her little secret mic above Hobart's desk, no one was taking any chances.

To the members of Operation Rainbow, she was still somewhat on probation. So they were taking extra precautions.

Eric typed in a few more commands, set his alarm to vibrate in one hour, and then he took a nap.

At the end of an hour, they woke up and undid their seatbelts. Michael pushed the button to open a little door on the side of the briefcase. Both exited and looked around. Seeing that it was clear, they went to work.

First, the two of them opened a side panel on the briefcase to reveal an array of tools, which included a fold-up extension ladder. They carried the ladder and placed it under the desk in the center. Michael went back to get some gear and strapped on a tiny tool belt full of gadgets.

He walked around the desk until he found the leg he was looking for and started to climb up. Meanwhile, Eric was setting up the ladder so it reached right up to the bottom of the desk. By now Michael had climbed up to the lion's head and looked around to see if Eric was ready. Eric has already climbed up the ladder and was waiting at the top. He gave Mike the thumbs-up signal, and Mike pushed on the two lion's eyes, and for his efforts got a *click*.

Eric ducked fast when the door under the desk dropped open and just barely missed his head. Then from his backpack he removed the key and inserted it into the lock. With a swift turn, it opened to reveal the wooden box Heather told them was there.

It was much too big for Eric to lug down by himself. So he rigged a string-and-pulley system he brought to the top of the ladder and lowered the box down to the floor. He shut the trap door, locked it, and then climbed down. With Mike's help, both of them carried the box over and secured it in the briefcase.

Next, they went around to the front of the desk where Mike again climbed one of the legs and made his way up on top of the massive desk. Once there, he lowered a string down to Eric, who tied the key on it. Mike then pulled it up. Using a letter opener found on the desk, he managed to open the drawer that Heather told them the key needed to be put back in.

Mike tossed the key at the slightly open drawer. It missed, bounced off the edge, and fell to the floor, nearly hitting Eric. Eric jumped out of the way, and his quick reflexes saved him from getting hit. But then the key and the string were down on the floor.

Eric got up from where he landed and motioned to Mike to wait. He then went to the equipment in the briefcase and came back with a bow and arrow. He tied the end of the string to the arrow and shot it up past Mike. As it passed Mike, he grabbed the string and let the arrow fall on the desk.

This time when Mike pulled the key up, he was extra careful, lowering it into the drawer.

Now he had to figure out how to untie the string from the key. He took the string and wrapped the loose end around the desk lamp stand. Then holding onto the string coming up from the key and the one coming around the lamp, he lowered himself into the drawer.

He then untied the key, took the two ends of the string, and lowered them down to the floor. Eric grabbed them and held them tight so that Mike could use them to climb down.

But before he climbed down, Mike remembered Janet's instructions about Hobart's computer. So he went over to the

desktop computer, moved the mouse, and sure enough the computer screen came to life just like Janet said it would.

He thought to himself, *How does she know this guy so well? She said he would not read the document, and he didn't. Then she told us he would leave his computer on, and he did. Wow, she's good at her job!*

Mike turned to see Eric jump up and land on the desk. He pointed to the computer screen, and Eric nodded in approval. Eric quickly pulled a data stick out of his backpack and walked around to the back of the computer where he found the USB port. After plugging in the data stick, he walked back around to where the mouse was. He then moved the curser on the screen over top of the icon that looked like a hawk and then pushed the left mouse button.

The screen blinked. They could hear the disk drive whirling around at a high speed, and then everything stopped.

Eric again went around to the back of the computer and retrieved the data stick. Both of them went over to where the string was, and using it, they descended to the floor. Once they were both safely down, they both grabbed the string, and by pulling it back under the desk, they managed to shut the drawer containing the key.

Mike pulled on one side of the string, and it came down. They packed everything back into their special briefcase. Eric used hand signals that they should eat the sandwiches they brought and get ready to wait out the night.

After they ate and started settling down for the night, Eric thought back over the events of the last few days.

The next morning, Randle Hobart was a man on a mission. He thought to himself, This is the best day of my life; I can feel the money in my pocket already! He called his office and told Heather that he had some things to do but that she was to call him as soon as Ms. Cook called or came in.

He then went to the car dealer and ordered a new, very expensive Rolls Royce. That done, he drove down to the yacht sales office and signed the contract on the boat he had been wanting for a long time, the one he blackmailed the president of Simms Shipping into selling him.

From there, he went back uptown to the office of Jamaica Prosperities and wrote them a check for the house in Jamaica he had always wanted to own. The salesman took the check to his manager to get his okay. The manager, seeing the name on the check, picked up the phone and made a call. "I have a check from Randle Hobart for twenty-two million," he said to the party on the other end of the phone. "I see! What should I do? Yes, I understand, and thank you!"

The manager hung up the phone and went back into the office where Hobart was waiting. Hobart, seeing the check in the manager's hand, asked, "Is there a problem?"

"No, not at all, sir!" the manager said as he handed the check to the sales clerk.

"Merely a formality. After all, it is a rather large amount. You understand of course?"

"Of course!" Hobart said. "As I told your man here, the funds will be available by the end of the week!"

"Very good, sir! I hope you enjoy your beautiful house in Jamaica!"

Hobart had just started going over all the legal papers and signing the contract for the house when he got a call from his office.

"Sir, Ms. Cook will be here in half an hour," Miss Baryl told him.

"Very good, I'll be there straight away," he informed her, and he rushed to get through the signing of all the paper work without reading them.

After she hung up the phone, Heather quickly went into Hobart's office, picked up the briefcase, carried it out, and set it

down beside her desk. When she had closed his office door, she went back to her chair and sat down.

"Are you two all right in there?" she whispered.

And from the briefcase, Michael replied, "Top of the morning to you. We are fine and ready to get out of this contraption, we are!"

"They will be arriving soon, so be patient!" she said.

Eric said, "Good morning, Miss Baryl. Would you mind turning this thing around and placing it right next to your desk? That way we can get out and stretch our legs under your desk, and if anyone comes, we can quickly jump back in."

"Oh! Of course! There. How's that?"

"That will work just fine, thank you!" Eric answered as they got out and stretched.

Although Hobart tried to hurry through the contract signing, it seemed to be taking too long. He checked his watch, and it read eleven thirty-two a.m. He had twenty-eight minutes to get back to his office and sign his biggest deal ever.

He thought to himself, *Let's see now, it will take about fifteen minutes from here to get to the office. Good! Plenty of time!*

He signed the last of the contracts for his Jamaica house and rushed out to his car, only to find it being picked up by a tow truck.

"What do you think you're doing?" he yelled at the driver.

The tow truck driver was a very large, burly man with no sense of humor. "I'm towing this here vehicle, I am!" he said.

"No! You can't do that! That's my car!" Hobart yelled again.

By then the car had been lifted up and secured to the back of the tow truck. The driver tore off a copy of the paper work he had filled out and handed it to Hobart. As he did, he pointed to the *No Parking* sign where Hobart's vehicle had been.

Hobart turned to look in amazement at the sign and said, "That was not there when I parked here!"

The driver just shrugged, got into his truck, and drove off with Hobart's car.

Hobart just stood there for a minute and watched his car go down the street. All of a sudden he looked at his watch—eleven forty-six a.m.—swore, and tried to hail a cab as he took out his phone and dialed his office.

"Mr. Hobart's office," Miss Baryl answered.

"It's me," he said. "I'm having trouble getting back to the office. Is she there?"

"Yes, sir, she has been here for about half an hour. Where are you?"

"I have to take a cab, but I will be there in fifteen minutes. Please get her to wait!" Hobart pleaded.

"I will do my best, sir!" Heather said.

She put down the phone, turned, and winked at Janet, who had been listening in on the conversation.

"He will never make it in time!"

Janet picked up the briefcase, and the two women went into Hobart's office. Once inside with the door closed, Janet announced, "Okay, guys, you can come out, and make your selves at home!"

They both came out slowly, stretching and yawning. Eric asked, "What happens next?"

Janet explained, "The taxi driver will take the long way here. That will take about twenty minutes. When Mr. Hobart arrives he will find…"

The cab ride was a nightmare. He could not get the driver to understand his directions. The fool went the wrong way and then had to retrace their route. They finally pulled up in front of the

corporate offices. Hobart just threw some money at the driver and ran inside.

As the cab pulled away from the curb, the driver spoke into a hidden microphone.

"He's just now entering the building, and he is mad!" Ed Barns removed his fake beard and laughed.

When the elevator doors opened to Hobart's office, he found that Miss Baryl was not at her desk. *She must be in my office with Ms. Cook,* he thought to himself. He crossed the room and entered his office only to find it empty! He went to his desk and dialed the receptionist.

"This is Randle, do you know where Ms. Cook is?"

"Yes, sir, Ms. Cook left at twelve oh one p.m.," she told him.

"What? She left? No!" He looked at his watch only to see that it was now twelve sixteen p.m. "Where is Ms. Baryl?" he asked.

"Ms. Baryl left the building, sir."

"What? She left? Where did she go?" he questioned.

"I'm afraid I don't know, sir."

"Well, do you know when she plans to return?" he inquired.

"I don't believe she will be returning, sir. She informed me she was retiring and would not be back."

"She what? Retired? No, she can't retire! Didn't she have another month to go?"

"That's all the information I have, sir. Will there be anything else?"

He didn't answer because he just looked at his desk and saw the contract was gone! Randle Hobart all of a sudden realized that he had failed, again. He slumped down in his chair. The phone slowly slipped out of his hand and fell to the floor.

His mind was spinning, and he couldn't think. He had to do something, but what? How could he get the Hawk people to come back with that contract?

Why did all these things have to go wrong just when he was about to pull off the biggest deal in the company's history? Why? He got up and started pacing the floor.

"I must think!" he said to himself. "I need a plan."

Just then he stopped dead in his tracks.

"Oh no! The check! I have to cover that check by Friday, but how? How can I get twenty-two million by Friday?"

He sat back down to think, but his head was still spinning from the realization that he lost that big deal. He thought and thought. Finally, an idea hit him. He jumped out of his chair and started pacing again, and then he stopped.

"That's it!" he said. "I'll do it!"

He went back to his desk and pushed the button for the receptionist. "Yes, sir?" she answered.

"Do you have a number for Ms. Cook, from Hawk Industries?" he asked

"Yes, sir, she left her card with Miss Baryl."

"Good, get her on the phone, and tell her I would like to talk to her straight away. Tell her that I have a much better deal for her!"

"Yes, sir, I'll get right on that."

Janet Cook was already at the airport, waiting on Scott and Conor to arrive with the jet when she received the call from Hobart's receptionist.

"Hello, yes, this is Janet Cook, who's calling please?"

"Ms. Cook, this is Mr. Hobart's receptionist, and he would like to talk to you about the offer you made."

"I'm afraid that offer is no longer on the table," Janet said.

"Yes, we understand that, but Mr. Hobart would like you to entertain a better offer."

"What sort of offer are we talking about?" asked Janet.

"I'm not at liberty to say. But if you would call Mr. Hobart at his office, I'm sure he will explain."

"Very well, I have a few minutes before my plane gets here. What is his private number?"

After the receptionist gave her the number, Janet called Conor in the jet. "Hi, Conor, well, he called with a better offer just like we thought. He is expecting me to call him back. Do you still want to do this? It will take a lot to pull it off!"

"I know, Janet, and I trust that you know how to proceed. So go ahead and do it the way you think is best for us, and remember he's very sneaky and slimy. So don't let him wiggle off the hook!"

"Okay, Conor, I'm on it! See you in a few minutes," Janet said.

She punched in a phone number on her cell, and when the party answered, she said, "We are ready to proceed. What is your answer? Very well, I have the contracts with me now and can be in your office in about thirty minutes."

Janet hung up in time to see the HJ500 pulling into a spot at the private jet terminal. She walked outside to meet Scott and Conor just as they opened the door and came down the steps.

"Well, how did it go?" Conor asked.

"Just as we thought it would. We have everything we wanted, including our little surprise!"

"Great!" Conor said. "Now we can move to the final stage and get these Tinys out of Ireland and home to Tennessee!"

"Hi, Mom," Brittany said as she poked her head out of the jet's door."

"Brittany! What are you doing here? you're supposed to be in school!"

"I asked her to fly over and join us. I was thinking our meeting later with Miss O'Rourke might go smoother if Brittany is there. You know, if she sees another young lady and not just me," Conor answered.

"I see, good idea."

THE TELLING

After they talked for a few minutes, Janet looked at her watch. "I need to get to the Hobart office building right away."

Conor smiled and pointed past her shoulder at the bright blue helicopter sitting nearby. "I thought you might need a flying carpet, so I arranged one!"

"Why, thank you, kind sir! You are adapting to your new life style very nicely!" she laughed as she turned and headed for the helicopter.

Hobart had arrived back at his office after lunch to find a new secretary sitting at Miss Baryl's old desk.

"Good afternoon, sir," she said.

He looked her over and then asked, "Is Ms. Cook in there?" as he pointed to the door of his office.

"No, sir."

He looked disturbed and said, "Well, when she arrives, send her right in."

"Yes, sir!"

Just then the door to the conference room across the hall opened, and out came the board of directors along with Ms. Cook. They all shook her hand and went their separate ways except for Ms. Cook and the chairman of the board.

Hobart was dumbstruck and just stood there outside his office with his mouth open.

Finally, the chairman came over to him and said, "Well, Randle, you finally did it! I can't say that you will be missed!" he laughed.

He turned and, as he left, remarked to Ms. Cook, "Thank you again. Have a nice trip back to the States."

"You are most welcome, and thank you!" she replied as she went over and pushed the up elevator button.

Hobart was still standing there, wondering what had just happened. "I thought we had a deal."

Janet turned to face him. "We never had a deal! The board of directors and I did. After they learned of the things you've been involved with, I believe they felt that you would no longer be needed at Hobart Industries."

With that, she walked up right in his face, leaned in close, and she whispered, so that the secretary couldn't hear, "And if you ever endanger my *little* friends again, we will destroy you completely! Do you understand?"

Hobart was so shocked by what he had just heard that he couldn't even answer.

Janet, seeing that the elevator has arrived, walked in and was gone.

Later in his office, Hobart was cleaning out his desk and getting ready to leave the company job he really didn't want in the first place. He was still in a state of confusion as to what just went wrong. He kept going over and over the past few days' events, trying to sort out all that had happened.

He opened the desk drawer where he kept the key; seeing that it was still there, he took it and crawled under his desk. To open the hidden door, he again pushed the lion's eyes. Once the door was opened, he quickly unlocked the safe. Fully expecting to just reach in and remove the box, he was thoroughly confused when he realized the safe was *empty*!

"What? How?" he yelled. "I've been robbed, but how? How did they know?"

Then it dawned on him. "Ms. Baryl! She is the only one who knew about the safe. She took the journal. I will call the police and have her picked up!"

He again called his secretary, but there was no answer. Then he called the receptionist desk.

"Yes, sir?" a new voice answered.

"Get the police over here straight away; I've been robbed!" Hobart said.

"Robbed? Good heavens, are you all right, sir?"

"No, I'm not all right; just call them *now*!" he yelled.

"Yes, sir, right away, sir!"

Only a minute later the receptionist buzzed the intercom. "Sir, the police are here to see you."

"Here already? Very good, send them in!" Hobart said.

As the police lieutenant and another officer entered his office, Hobart stood and came around his desk to meet them. "Good, you're here…" he started to say when the officer grabbed him by the arm. Before he knew what was going on, he had both his arms behind him in handcuffs.

"What is all this?" Hobart asked.

"You're under arrest!"

"Arrest for what?"

The lieutenant pulled out his pad and opened it up to check his notes. "Let's see what we have here, accessory to assault, involuntary manslaughter, invasion of privacy, writing bad checks, and attempted extortion. Now come along quietly. That's a good boy!"

Back at the airport, the guys had the corporate jet fueled and ready to go. Janet had just arrived and climbed aboard.

Conor asked, "So what about Randle Hobart? Is that all taken care of?"

"Yes! He is all wrapped up and tied with a bow, or better still, handcuffs!"

With her last comment, they all laughed and then Conor announced, "Well then, let's go finish *Operation Rainbow*!"

Bring Them Home

In Ireland, a van driven by Conor was on its way to a very important meeting. Sitting beside him were the two Tinys from Tennessee, Eric and Bryan. They were on their way to make first contact with the Irish Tinys, and the Irish benefactor Katelyn O'Rourke. In the back seat, Brittany was anxious about meeting the girl from Ireland.

As they drove through the Irish streets, Eric was thinking about how, tonight, he would finally get to meet Michael, the Irish Tiny. He was concerned about Bryan and himself making their first contact with Katelyn.

Conor pulled over to the curb and stopped the van. Eric stood up in the passenger seat and looked out the window to see a misty rain falling and the fog was thickening.

They had a few minutes to wait until the prearranged time to make contact. Eric and Bryan get out of the van, Conor parked about a block away and on the opposite side of the street from the O'Rourke house. Through the fog and drizzling rain, the streetlights were dimly glowing, making visibility very limited.

The two Tinys took a long look around to see if any Bigs were about, but on a rainy night like this, they doubted it. Seeing it was clear, Eric gave Conor, who was looking down at them from the driver's side window, the thumbs up, and they started out.

Eric turned to Bryan. "Stay close and alert. I don't like being this close to so many Bigs!"

Bryan, who had been looking forward to this adventure, was about to burst with excitement. "I've got your back, bro!"

As they moved down the street toward the O'Rourke house, they could hear the big people, in their homes, getting ready for the evening meal. They heard the children running as parents called them to come and eat.

Eric thought of his home back in Tennessee, some three thousand miles from there. *I hope I didn't bite off more than I can chew by taking on this assignment,* he thought to himself.

Now that they were right across from the O'Rourke house, Eric stopped. They must cross the street and go behind the house as per their instructions. Neither of them has crossed this large of a paved street on foot before. To them it looked like a mile of wide-open ground. Here was where they could be easily seen or maybe have a car come along. Now that wouldn't be good!

Conor had driven around the area a few times to make sure that no one was watching the house. So right now, Eric's only concern was with this wide-open space they called a street.

"Are you ready for a run?" he asked his brother.

"I'm ready! Let's go!" answered Bryan, and off they ran.

When they got about halfway across, they heard a dog bark! Eric and Bryan both froze. After realizing that it was coming from way down the street, they continued on, this time even faster.

As they reached the curb, Eric announced, "Dogs, I don't like dogs!" He panted.

Bryan, catching his breath, remarked, "The dog we met on our trip back from the lake was nice, and he really liked Dina!"

They both remembered the big lick the dog gave Dina and laughed.

"Okay! Let's get around to the back and find that dog house," Eric directed.

They moved out one at a time, first Eric and then Bryan, covering each other as they moved from one bush to another. They worked their way very close the doghouse when from nearby, a small voice said, "You lads look like you've done this before!" It was Michael standing in a bush not far from the doghouse. "I assume you must be the lads from America!" he continued, and he stepped out to greet them.

Eric came over, held out his hand, and shook Michael's. "Yes, I'm Eric, and this is my brother Bryan."

Michael beamed a smile from ear to ear, and you could hear the relief in his voice as he said, "Suren, it's a joy to see the likes of you two lads! If you will follow me, I will take you to meet Miss O'Rourke who waits for us inside."

They followed Michael around to the back of the phony doghouse, through the false door, and inside where they found a toy train sitting on its track.

Michael walked over to it and climbed onto one of the empty flatbed cars. As he sat down, he told the guys, "Climb aboard, lads! It's only a short ride into the house from here."

They both looked at each other, shrugged, and climbed on.

As Michael pushed a button, the train started down the track and into a tunnel. When it entered the pitch-black tunnel, its headlight came on. They dropped down a steep slope that took them under the yard then back up another slope and into the house.

As they came to a stop, Eric noticed that they were now inside a false wall. Michael jumped off the train, and the guys followed him. He walked about five feet inside this false wall until he came to a small door; he opened it and stepped through. The guys followed. The first thing they saw was that they were standing under a kitchen sink inside the sink cabinet.

Bryan looked around and said, "Now, that's a clever way to get inside!"

Michael smiled and said, "The first time I rode that contraption into the tunnel, I was a wee bit frightened until the light turned on!"

Katelyn O'Rourke was sitting at the kitchen table, waiting, when she heard the Tinys talking from under the sink. Michael opened the cabinet door, and the three of them stepped out onto the kitchen floor.

Michael was the first to speak. "Katelyn, may I present Eric and Bryan from America!"

Katelyn knelt down on the floor and held out her hands to greet them. The two Tiny men, seeing the bright smile on her face and the tears in her eyes, knew right away they had found another friend! They both came over to her, and each took hold of a hand.

Eric announced, "Miss O'Rourke, it is indeed a pleasure to meet you. We have heard so many good things about you."

Bryan piped in, "Yeah, but they didn't tell us that you were so pretty!"

They all laughed.

Michael said, "I think we had better go now. I don't believe the house is being watched, but I don't want to take any chances. Katelyn, if you will go out the side door and come around to the backyard, we will go back the way we came and meet you by the doghouse."

"Okay!" she said as she got up, grabbed her purse, and went out the door. The three Tinys hurried back under the sink and through the secret door that lead down the false wall to the train. Once they are all onboard, Michael pushed another button, and off they went back to the doghouse.

When they got outside, they found Katelyn waiting for them.

Eric directed, "Everyone wait here while I go around to the front of the house and see if it's all clear."

And off he ran. A few moments later, he came back and announced, "It looks okay. Let's go!"

Once they reached the van, Eric said, "Katelyn, please get in the passenger seat, and us three will ride in the back seat."

With that, they all piled in. As they closed the doors, Eric said, "Katelyn and Michael, may I introduce you to our benefactor, Conor O'Brien and Miss Brittany Cook."

"Nice to meet you!" Conor said as he shook her hand while grinning from ear to ear at this strikingly beautiful, red-headed young woman.

From the back seat, Brittany said, "Hi, Katelyn, did you get my e-mail?"

"Yes, I did, and thank you for coming with Mr. O'Brien."

"Nice to finally meet you, Mr. O'Brien," Katelyn said, smiling back at Conor.

When the handshaking continued for some time, Bryan interrupted, "Isn't she pretty, Conor?"

"Yes, she is!" Conor replied.

But when the four in the back seat all started laughing, the spell was broken, and the two in the front seat stopped shaking hands.

Michael remarked, "We had better move along. I don't like being out in the open like this."

Conor turned back to the steering wheel, started the van, and then asked Katelyn, "Do you mind if we take you to where we have the plane and the rest of our team?"

"No, not at all!" Katelyn answered. "I'm excited to meet the others so that I can thank you all for what you are doing."

"Good, then fasten your seat belts. Here we go!" Conor said as he drove away from the O'Rourke house and headed back to the hanger where the other members of the Rainbow team were waiting.

From the shadows of a house across the street, a man had been watching and waiting. After a few minutes, the dark figure

appeared and moved quietly from shadow to shadow, working his way down the street and around the corner to where his car awaited. Once inside, he picked up his cell phone, dialed as he started the car, and drove off. When he heard the party he had called answer, he said, "The package has been picked up and is on its way."

"Any problems?" asked the person on the other end of the line.

"None," was the reply.

"Okay, then I'll see you at the hanger," Scott said.

"I'll be around, but you won't see me!" laughed Ed.

As the gang was driving along, Conor said, "I'm very sorry that we didn't get here sooner before your uncle…"

Before he could finish, Katelyn reached over and touched his arm. "It's all right, Mr. O'Brien, you came as soon as you knew what was going on, and I'm most grateful!"

"Thank you, but please call me Conor. My father was Mr. O'Brien!"

"All right, but you must call me Katelyn or Kate, if you please!"

Most of the trip to the airport and to the rented hanger was quiet. Everyone was deep in thought with concerns about what had to be done the next day. Except Conor who couldn't stop thinking about what a beautiful woman Katelyn was. *I wonder if she has a boyfriend.*

He kept trying to get another look at her, but in the dark van it was too hard to see. The van drifted toward the right side of the road. *Oops! I had better concentrate on my driving. It's the left lane over here, isn't it?*

Katelyn is also doing some thinking. *He's very young to be the head of such a large, important company, and the benefactor of the little ones, as well! I'll bet he's about the same age as me, I didn't expect that he would be so cute!!*

In the back seat, Bryan had been wondering, *How many more Tinys are here in Ireland?*

And Eric was thinking, *When will we meet the rest of the Tinys? I hope there are plenty of girls!*

Finally, they arrived at the hanger. As they approached the side door, they saw someone dressed in black, standing by the entrance, but they couldn't make out who it is.

Conor pulled up closer, and when he turned the van toward the side of the hanger, the headlights showed them that it was Scott who had been keeping an eye open for them. As they parked, Scott came over to the van and helped Katelyn with her door. "You must be Katelyn!" he said as he held open the van door and offered his hand to help her step down. "Hi, I'm Scott."

"Pleased to meet you," she said.

As she got out of the van, he led her through the side door of the hanger. Inside, where the others were waiting, she saw Heather Baryl. She ran over and gave her a big hug. Katelyn stepped back. "I'm so glad to see you!"

Heather could hardly contain the tears. "I'm glad to see you too!"

Conor took Katelyn's hand and led her over to meet Janet. "Janet Cook, meet Katelyn O'Rourke."

"I'm very pleased to finally meet you, Miss O'Rourke. Would you and Ms. Baryl join Brittany and I upstairs in the living quarters while the men get the jet ready for tomorrow?" Janet said.

Conor announced, "Later on I would like to show you around, and we can talk, if you wouldn't mind?"

As the ladies were walking up the stairs, Katelyn stopped and replied, "I would like that very much, Conor."

And then she turned and continued on up to the living quarters. Conor just stood there, watching her with this silly smile on his face until Bryan broke in with "I don't know about the rest of you, but I'm hungry, and I could use a bathroom break!"

Conor snapped out of his trance. "That sounds like a very good idea, Bryan. Let's all go up and join the ladies for some refreshments. We can check the plane after we get something to eat."

So they all went up and joined the ladies.

Later, after Conor and Scott had gone over the complete checklist on the jet and had everything ready for the next day's getaway, they went upstairs to find the ladies sitting around the dining table with tea and coffee. Conor asked Katelyn, "Would you like to join me for a tour of the airplane?"

As he was showing her the plane with all the instrument panels and test equipment on it, Katelyn asked, "How are you going to have room for all the little ones in here with all this?"

Conor took her over to one of the instrument panels that was about in the middle of the plane; then he reached down under one of the panel corners and hit a button. With a click it opened to reveal what looked like seats from an airliner, except these were small and just the right size for a Tiny to sit in.

When she saw this, she looked back at him and asked, "How in the world did you arrange to do that?"

"I have my resources." He grinned. "We were also able to install two functioning bathrooms that are the appropriate size for our little friends. Scott even added some drink dispensers, and, oh yeah, each seat has a pillow and blanket."

"How did you manage to make all these little things?" Katelyn asked.

"One of the companies we own is a toy manufacturer," he explained.

After closing the panel, he took her hand and led her back out of the plane and over to an office at the back of the hanger. Inside the office area was a small waiting room, and as they entered it, he said, "I believe you and I have a lot to discuss. I know it's late,

but there's so much I want to know about you and that I want to tell you about us. Do you mind if we talk for a while?"

"I don't mind at all, but how will I get back to the house?"

"Oh, I forgot to tell you, or show you, this place has plenty of bedrooms, and the ladies have made one up for you and Brittany. That is if you wish to stay. I don't want you to think we're holding you here or anything like that!" Conor said.

"Oh, no! I don't feel that way at all! You all have been so very nice to me. I don't know how to start to thank you for what you're doing for the little ones," she said.

"So you will stay?" he asked.

"Yes, I would like that very much. I want to know all about the little ones in America. And you and your family," she said as she settled back in her chair.

Conor and Katelyn talked for hours that night. They found out that they both felt a great need to care for the Tinys and how they each loved these little gifts from God and how much their lives have changed since meeting them.

They both liked a lot of the same things, and neither one cared too much for the rich life but instead liked things a bit simpler.

She was worried about not being able to see them anymore. He assured her she could come and visit anytime. He told her all about his grandparents and how and where they lived. She thought it sounded like a nice place.

After talking for a while, Conor realized for the first time that Katelyn's last name, O'Rourke, was the same as his great-great-grandmother's. The realization hit him like a brick! He was beginning to really like her, and now it occurred to him they could be related!

He had to ask her, but how without letting her know how he was starting to like her? After worrying about it for some time, he finally just came out with it.

"Kate, I have been wondering about something."

"Oh! What is it?" she asked.

"It's your maiden name, O'Rourke. My great-great-grandmother was an O'Rourke, and I was just thinking…"

She laughed out loud and said, "If you're thinking we're related, you can stop worrying about it!"

"Huh! How?" he asked.

"I'm not an O'Rourke!" she announced.

"You're not, but you told everyone you were…" he questioned.

"What I mean to say is I was adopted. I took my adoptive parents' name. I'm a Kelly by birth," she said.

"Kelly? You mean you're not an O'Rourke?"

"Yes! I mean no! I'm not!"

He jumped up and started dancing around yelling, "Kelly, Kelly, Kelly what a wonderful name!"

She was laughing, and he was dancing when Scott and Janet came in to see what all the fuss was about. "What is going on?" asked Janet.

Kate was laughing so hard at Conor dancing she couldn't answer her. Finally, Conor stopped dancing, came over, and shook Scott's hand and said, "She's not really an O'Rourke!" and then he plopped down beside Kate.

Scott looked at the two of them grinning and blushing and then back at Janet. "What in the world are you talking about?" Scott asked.

"You don't get it, do you? I thought she was an O'Rourke. But she's a Kelly, not an O'Rourke."

Conor explained that he was worried about Kate and him being related through his great-great-grandmother.

After they all have a good laugh about it, Janet and Scott stayed for a while, and the four of them went over their plans for getting the Tinys out of Ireland.

It must have been around four in the morning, everyone else had long since gone to bed, when he finally got up enough nerve to ask her to come back with them.

"That way you can see for yourself just how they'll live. How we all take care of them. You would get to meet my grandparents and see Tennessee! So what do you think?" he blurted out all at once.

She was beginning to really like this O'Brien fellow more than she thought was possible in such a short time. She did not want any of them to go. So maybe going with them was not such a bad idea.

"I need to think it over and get some sleep. Can I let you know in the morning?" she said with a yawn.

He had not realized just how late it was until she yawned. So did he, and they both laughed.

"I think you're right. Let's get some rest, and then we can talk some more tomorrow, or should I say today?"

Conor showed her to the room. As they said good night, he looked at her and said, "I know we have only just met and hardly know each other, Katelyn, but I really would like the opportunity to get to know you better."

"Me too," she said, and she gave him a big sleepy smile.

"Good night!" They both said at the same time.

After breakfast the next morning, they all went downstairs to the hanger. The guys were getting the van ready to go pick up all of the Tinys and bring them back here to the hanger while the ladies were making sure the secret compartment in the airplane for the Tinys had plenty of water and prepared food for the trip.

When it looked like everything was in order, Katelyn went over to Conor and asked, "How many trips will you have to make in the van to get all of the Tinys and their things?"

Conor wiped off his hands with the rag he had in his back pocket after checking the engines for the fourth time. "Well, after talking to Michael, we estimate it will take four to five trips, three to bring most of the people and at least two loads for their belongings," he answered.

"What are you going to do about their belongings? I don't think you have room in the plane for the people and their things?" Kate questioned.

"You're right! We were thinking of shipping them as airfreight. But I must admit I didn't give that part of this move much thought. We don't have any crates or boxes here to pack them in," said Conor.

Katelyn thought for a minute and then said, "I can make a call and have a truck full of crates here in about one hour."

"You can? Oh, yeah, I forgot you have a shipping company right near here. What a great idea, thanks!"

So when Conor and the three Tinys left in the van, Katelyn made her call, and started things rolling.

Michael had arranged for the Irish Tinys to meet them on a back road in the woods nearest the caves where they lived. The old dirt road was dry and dusty from lack of rain the past month or so. Conor had to drive slower than he would have liked just to try to keep the dust down.

As they neared the spot Michael had picked, he gave directions to Conor where to stop. "Just after the big Oak tree on the right," he said as he pointed.

"Okay! I see it," Conor answered, and he pulled over to stop just past the big Oak. As the dust from the road settled, Michael opened the side door and jumped down to the ground. He took a good look around, but he couldn't see anyone. He was starting to wonder, *What could have gone wrong for them not to be here?* When

GARY E. REAVIS, SR.

from up in the Oak he heard, "Well, if it isn't Michael Flanagan himself! Top of the morning, Michael!"

Michael looked up to see Shawn Dugan, the leader of their little group, smiling down at him from one of the branches.

Michael said, "And to you as well, Shawn Dugan. Are the others here with you?"

"Aye! That they are my boy! That they are!" Shawn said.

With that, he put his fingers to his lips and whistled. Out from behind every tree and bush came the Tinys. Men, women, and children, all two hundred of them carrying as much as they could. As they all gathered around the old Oak tree, Conor got out of the van along with Eric and Bryan.

Eric came around the front of the van, and as he got closer, he saw all of them. He stopped, and with tears in his eyes, he lowered his head to say a soft prayer. "Thank you, Lord God, for these special gifts you have placed in our care. I ask for your help this day as we bring them to a new home in Tennessee. Amen!"

All the Tinys said, "Amen!"

Michael came over with Shawn, who had climbed down from the tree, and introduced him to Conor, Eric, and Bryan. Then Conor said, "We must hurry and get them into the van!"

Flight Home

Ed and Conor had parked the HK500 as near to the customs office as he could. They had been waiting for about an hour for the customs and security team to come out and go over the aircraft so that they could get their clearance to depart Ireland. Ed had ordered an auxiliary power and air-conditioning unit be attached to the plane. The test equipment had to be kept running and not allowed to overheat. Finally the customs official arrived and came aboard.

Ed spotted him approaching and got out his checklist and was going over each item with Conor when the customs official entered the plane.

"Customs," was all the man said, and then he started looking around at all the test equipment. Then he went up to the front of the plane. Conor had installed seats for six passengers right behind the cockpit along with a bathroom. The built-in storage compartment was stacked full of cables and spare parts for the test equipment.

As the custom official looked around, he asked Ed, "How many people?"

"Five plus the pilot," Ed answered nonchalantly.

"Names please," the customs official asked just as the security officer arrived. When the officer boarded the plane, he brought along a very large German Sheppard. The officer looked at the customs official and then at Ed. Ed nodded to the security officer, giving him the okay to start their search for drugs or weapons. Ed turned his attention back to the customs official, and as he identified each person, he pointed to them. "Scott Curtis, our chief

engineer; Janet Cook, the corporation's CEO and her daughter, Brittany; Katelyn O'Rourke, our Ireland division CEO; this is Conor O'Brien, the owner; and myself, I'm—"

The man held up his hand and said, "We know who you are, Mr. Barns." He looked past Ed at the security officer who had just finished his sweep of the plane. He gave him the thumbs-up sign. "If you will just sign here please, that will be all we need."

Ed signed the paperwork. The security officer and the German Sheppard left the plane, followed shortly by the customs official. Ed closed the door and let out a sigh. "Well, that was fast!" As he walked up to the cockpit, he told everyone to get in their seats and buckle up. Once he got into the pilot's seat, he fired up the engines, put on his earphones, and when he received permission from the tower, he said, "Hang on everyone, we're outta here!"

He pushed the throttles forward, and the jet moved down the runway like it was shot out of a cannon! At one hundred fifty knots, Ed rotated the nose, and they headed skyward like a rocket. Once they reached cruising altitude, he set the autopilot and then turned to Conor. "Why don't you take it for a while so I can take a break." Conor climbed into the pilots seat and announced over the intercom, "Okay, folks, you can get out of your seats if you want to and move around. Katelyn, if you would like to see the view from up here, please join me in the cockpit."

After Katelyn, Brittany, and Janet helped show some of the Tinys where they could get refreshments and where the bathrooms were, Katelyn joined Conor up front.

As she entered, Conor pointed to the co-pilot's seat, and she very carefully climbed into it and sat down. After looking around the cockpit, she looked out the window and down at the ocean. "How high are we?" she asked.

Conor pointed to the flat panel where the airspeed, altitude, and heading were displayed and told her, "Twenty-three thousand feet right now. They will keep us at this altitude for about three more hours then we will start our descent into US airspace."

Katelyn had followed Conor when he pointed to the instruments and was still studying the flat panel. After a bit she said, "We are traveling at six hundred thirty miles per hour on a heading of two sixty-five, and we are two thousand, six hundred fifty-nine miles from our destination, is that correct?"

Conor looked at her and just beamed! "You know how to fly?" he asked.

"No, but I have read about airplanes, and flying has been one of my interests since I was old enough to remember."

He turned in his seat to face her and said with a big smile on his face, "Wow, will you be my girlfriend?"

She threw her head back and laughed.

Back in the cabin, most of the Tinys were getting used to the plane. Some of them were getting out of their seats, moving around and talking to each other. Eric and Bryan were helping those who asked how to use the drink dispenser and where the restrooms were.

Bryan was busy talking to some of the teenagers that had gathered around him. Eric was just kind of standing off to one side when a young Tiny lady came up to him. "I was wondering if one of you lads wouldn't mind showing me the rest of the plane?" she said.

Eric, realizing this pretty young lady was talking to him, snapped out of his daydream and said, "I would be glad to show you around if you like. My name is Eric."

"I know, and that is your younger brother Bryan over there," she said. "I'm Drea, and I would be pleased if you would show me around."

Just then Michael's younger sister ran up, "Can I come with you?"

"Eric, this is Michael's sister, Lena," Drea said grudgingly, thinking to herself, *I found this one; go find your own.* "No! You can't come with us. Go over there and find out what Bryan is doing with the other kids," Drea demanded as she took Eric's

hand, and they headed for the open test panel that led out into the rest of the aircraft.

As Eric was taking Drea around to see the different areas of the plane, they met Shawn, who had been looking around by himself. As they came up to Shawn, Drea said as she pointed to the cockpit door, "Father, why don't you go look in there?"

Eric thought to himself, *So that's who she is, the daughter of the Irish leader, hmmm.*

Shawn reached up to scratch his beard, nodded, and headed for the front of the plane.

Drea again took Eric's hand and headed for the back of the plane where they ran into Michael and Drew who had also been looking around. Michael introduced Drew to Eric. "Drew, I would like you to meet Eric, from America. He is the head scout, and, Eric, this is Drew, my intended."

"Intended?" questioned Eric.

"I believe in America you would say fiancée," Drea adds.

"Oh! Glad to meet you!" Eric said. "Are you enjoying the flight?"

"Yes, very much!" Drew answered. "This is the first time I have ever flown. As for that matter, it is the first time for all of us from Ireland. Is it not?" she questioned as she looked at Michael.

"Yes, it is, and a very exciting thing this flying!" said Michael. "Have you been flying much before?" he asked Eric.

"No, the trip over here was my first time," Eric said.

Drea asked, "How long will it take to get there?"

Eric thought for a minute then said, "I don't know, but it did take about six hours when we flew over here. So, I would assume that it'd be about the same time for the return trip. Would you two like to join us in the back?" He pointed at the place where the test equipment cabinets ended just before the aft bulkhead of the aircraft, leaving an open area of floor about three feet by four feet. "I saw a blanket up front that was not being used. I'll go get it and make a soft place to sit," he said as he ran off to get it. While he was gone, Drew looked at Drea.

"He is very nice, isn't he, Drea."

"Yes, he is and cute too!" Drea said, and the three of them laughed.

Eric returned with the blanket, and they all helped fold it into a soft sitting area. All four of them sat down and started getting acquainted.

Meanwhile, Shawn Dugan had gone up to the front of the plane to see the cockpit. As he entered and saw all the instruments and switches, he exclaimed, "How in the world do you know where to look or what to push?"

Conor looked around to see Shawn standing slightly behind and in between the pilot and co-pilot seats. "Why don't you come on in and climb up in the co-pilot's seat with Katelyn and have a look around?"

"Yes! Come on up here with me and see this wonderful view!" Katelyn exclaimed.

"Now I wouldn't want to bother you while you're driving this thing!" Shawn said.

"It's okay! You're not bothering me, and besides, I'm not driving right now anyway," Conor added.

"You're not? Then who in blazes is?" asked Shawn.

"The auto pilot is doing all the flying right now. I'm just keeping an eye on things," Conor said.

"Auto pilot, you say, and just what is this auto pilot you be talking about? All I see is you two just sitting here and neither one of you have hold of that steering thing?" Shawn asked as he climbed up into the seat with Katelyn, turned around, and looked out the windshield just as a little cloud passed by. He looked out the side window and down at the sea below. Then he looked back at Conor and smiled. "Tis a wonder this flying machine, is it not?"

"Aye, it is that," Katelyn said almost in a whisper.

Back in the seating area for the Tinys, Bryan had become the hero of the children. Of course he had shown them where

the goodies that Conor, Scott, and the ladies put onboard for all to enjoy.

The thing the kids liked most was pop. Root beer and orange turned out to be on the top of the request list. Candies came in a close second. Their parents all had sandwiches and milk or tea.

After he filled up the kids with goodies, he took them to the back where he showed them a flat, box-like machine. When he pushed the button in the front of it, it opened up. What the children saw inside were all these squares with letters and numbers on them, and in just a few seconds, pictures started appearing on the inside of the lid. All you hear from the kids was ohs and ahs; Bryan was smiling from ear to ear. Next he pushed a few buttons and then, using the mouse-pad, moved the cursor over on top of a picture on the screen, and when he pushed another button, magic happened.

On the computer screen was a video of the Tinys' village in Jamestown Tennessee and greetings from the Tennessee Tinys. After that, he spent the next hour or so answering all their questions.

Soon it was time to start their approach to the Nashville airport.

Conor announced over the intercom, "Well, it's time to get ready to land. So, will you all please return to your seats? Scott, make sure we are all buttoned up and ready for the customs. Let's pray that it goes as smooth as it did in Ireland. Now once we stop, everyone must be very quiet and still until I say it is okay." After his announcement, Ed took over the controls and, he became very busy talking to traffic control and the airport tower for landing instructions.

The landing was smooth as silk. They were given permission to park outside the Hawk Industries hanger to wait for the customs people there. Once the customs official boarded, he looked over the paperwork from Ireland then checked the inside of the plane and everyone's IDs. He had Ed sign a form, said good afternoon, and he was gone.

Janet had called ahead to have a motor home waiting for them in the hanger. The plane was towed into the hanger and the doors shut. By the time the ground crew had secured the aircraft, it was getting late. Ed told the ground crew that they could go on home, and in the morning they would download all the results of the test. So when the last of the crew had left, it was dark outside. The only ones in the hanger were the six Bigs and the Tinys who were still in the jet.

Scott, Brittany and Janet checked all offices to make sure they were empty. Conor and Katelyn started helping the Tinys transfer from the plane to the RV. Once they were all inside the RV, Scott, Janet and Brittany said their good-byes. Ed, Conor and Katelyn drove the RV the ninety-six miles to Grandpa's house just outside of Jamestown.

As they drove up to the house, Conor saw Grandpa and Grandma waiting on the front porch. When they had come to a stop, Conor reached up and turned on the interior lights and announced, "We are finally at your new home; welcome to America!"

The Tinys were all whooping, hollering, and some were dancing with joy.

As they all climbed out of the RV, waiting for them was Graybeard with about twenty of the Tennessee Tinys ready to greet them and guide them to their new homes in the woods of Tennessee. Conor, seeing that Graybeard and crew had everything under control, took Katelyn by the hand and led her up to the porch.

"Grandpa, Grandma, I would like you to meet Katelyn O'Rourke from Ireland.

When the two grandparents came in from the porch, Conor looked back over his shoulder as he and Kate headed for the kitchen and said, "Oh, by the way, she isn't really an O'Rourke; she's a Kelly!" And the two of them laughed.

Ed Barns

The next morning all the Operation Rainbow team were at Conor's grandparents' house. Grandma had made a big breakfast for everyone. They all found a seat at the table. Before they dug in, Grandpa bowed his head, and the others did the same. All except Ed, who was kind of caught off guard, but when Grandpa started saying grace, Ed figured out what was going on, and he too bowed his head. Grandfather' prayed, "Heavenly Father, we give you thanks for your bounty and ask you to bless the hands that prepared it. We thank you for Janet, Brittany, Scott and Ed, and our newest member, Katelyn, who you have sent to help us in taking care of our little friends. We ask for your guidance as we try to do each task set before us the best we can, remembering always your grace is sufficient! Amen!"

All through the meal Ed kept going over those words in his head. He had never heard anyone pray like that before. He was confused and a little curious about what was meant by "your grace is sufficient."

He usually felt very uncomfortable and uneasy around religious nuts. That was what he used to call people like that. The ones that read the Bible, prayed, and things like that. But here he felt a kind of peacefulness and right at home.

He had known after only a few days that Conor, Scott, and Janet were Christians. Strangely, he had not been put out by it. Despite what he had been led to believe in his upbringing, no one here had shoved a Bible in his face or called him a sinner! On the

contrary, they had accepted him from the beginning, treated him like he was family, and he liked that. He liked it a lot!

Later, after everyone pitched in and helped Grandma with cleaning up the kitchen, Ed found Grandpa out on the front porch all by himself, sitting in his favorite chair. Ed joined him and after sitting down in one of the rockers, he began, "Can I ask you a question about what you said at the table?"

Grandpa looked over at him with that smile that set people at ease. "Sure, Ed, shoot."

Ed looked down at his hands in his lap and said, "I don't know much about the Bible, and I wasn't taught about God and such…" He hesitated.

"Go on, son, what's on your mind?"

"Well, when you said, 'your grace is sufficient,' what did you mean by that?"

"The scriptures tell us we're saved by the grace of God. When Jesus died on the cross for all our sins—passed, present, and future—that was enough. The debt of our sins was paid for. We only need to confess that we have sinned, accept God's gift of forgiveness, and ask the Lord to come into our hearts! In other words, through God's grace, the work on the cross is sufficient! We are forgiven!" Grandpa proclaimed.

Deep in thought for some time, Ed finally said, "Thank you for explaining it. I have never heard it put like that before."

Grandpa continued, "Let me paraphrase it this way: He knows where you've been, and He knows what you've done, and He still loves you and wants you to come home!"

Ed just sat there with a tear in his eye.

Grandpa got up. "When you're ready, son, just talk to Him. He knows your heart!"

Grandpa started to go in the house but stopped when Ed told him, "I don't believe God can forgive me!"

Grandpa came back over and placed a hand on Ed's shoulder, "Son, He already has! You just need to accept His forgiveness."

"But I've done terrible things! How can He forgive me?" Ed announced in anger, "I'm afraid He won't forgive what I've had to do!"

Sitting back down and after a short, silent prayer, Grandpa said, "Fear of God is a good thing. It shows that you respect God as being the almighty! But He is also a loving God, the one who created us and wants us to fellowship with Him. You see, Ed, God is able to forgive and to forget our sins! We try to forget things, but we cannot, but God can! Whatever you have done, God will forgive!"

Grandpa reached over and picked up his Bible and opened it, and after searching through a few verses, he said, "Ah! Here it is in Isaiah. Here's what God has to say about your sins! Isaiah one, eighteen.

"'Come now, let us reason together,' said the Lord. 'Though your sins are like scarlet, they shall be white as snow; though they are red as crimson, they shall be like wool.'"

Ed thought about what Grandpa had said for a while; Grandpa just sat and waited for him. Finally, Ed asked, "What do I need to do or say?"

Grandpa quietly answered, "That's the easy part, son. It's called the sinner's prayer, and it goes something like this, 'Lord I have sinned. Please forgive me and come into my heart!'"

Ed lowered his head and quietly asked God to forgive him. To let him have the peace that he saw in these people.

Free-Dome

Three months later in Tennessee...

The siren went off and could be heard all over town. People were running everywhere, trying to get to the safety of the buildings. Once inside, window shutters were being slammed, locks were being thrown on the heavy doors. On the outskirts of town was what looked like a military compound that held four buildings, a sign over the gate read Rangers. The sign on the first building read Barracks. On the second it read, Headquarters. The third building's sign was Dining Hall, and the forth, Command Center.

About thirty young men all dressed alike were running from different parts of the compound to fall into formation in front of the barracks. They all wore form-fitting camouflage uniforms with knee-high, lace-up moccasins. Around their waists was a belt, and each belt had two pouches and a large knife. On their backs each had a bow and quiver of arrows. Each wore their hair differently; longhair tied back in ponytails, others shoulder length, and still some had their heads shaved. Every ranger had a communication headset on with a microphone placed in front of their mouth.

The door to the headquarters building flew open. Standing in the doorway was the captain dressed the same, but on his belt hung a knife, two pouches, and four smoke grenades. His hair was dark red and tied back in a ponytail.

"Squads four and five secured the town. No one on the streets until we sound the all clear!" he commanded as he descended the stairs. Ranger squads four and five broke formation and headed

for three vehicles parked next to the main gate, and quickly they were on their way

"Communications, give me an update."

"Communications here, Cap. We have three high-flying intruders coming in from the east of town, flying fast and erratic, over."

"Copy that, keep me advised if there's any change in direction, Ranger one out," the captain said.

"Will do, Cap, out" was the reply.

"Remaining squads mount up!" the captain ordered.

The rangers climbed on to a large truck with a flat bed. The driver was already behind the wheel as the captain climbed in and said, "Head to the east of town!"

They skirted the outside of town then took a right and headed due east past a row of homes. They had not gone far when the captain ordered, "Stop!" then over his shoulder as he stepped out, "Rangers, dismount!" The men seemed to move as one, jumping down and forming into squads.

"Squad leaders, front and center!"

Three men stepped forward in responses to his command.

"The three of you are the only ones to fire and only on my signal, is that clear? I want everyone else notched and ready in case this thing goes sour."

"Yes, sir" was their reply.

"We don't have much time. Second squad, take the left of the field. Third squad, go to the right. First, spread out in the center. Everyone at twenty-foot intervals and stay alert! Move out!" the captain ordered.

Moments later, the captain heard in his ear peace, "All squads in position, sir!"

"Copy that," he replied.

His eyes were watching the sky to the east. Then he saw them. Three dots getting bigger and bigger the closer they got. It only took him a few seconds to determine what they were. Wasps!

With at least three-inch wingspans! They were a quarter the size of his Tiny rangers.

"Here they come. Stand by!" the captain said as he pulled two grenades from his belt. These were not ordinary smoke grenades; they are filled with a chemical that attracted insects.

"I hope it works on wasps like Conor said it would!" he said as he pulled the pin and tossed the two canisters as close to the center of the field as he could. There were two loud pops, and green smoke began to stream out from both of them. The reactions from the wasps took only moments. It was so fast it seemed unreal. Sensing the chemical, they zeroed in on the field and dove with lightning speed landing softly in the smoke.

The captain whispered into his mic, "Squad leaders, target the nearest wasp to your position. On my mark."

He watched as the wasps searched the ground for whatever the chemical made them think was there. "Fire!" he commanded.

Three arrows shot into the field two of them striking their targets. Instantly the creatures went stiff then collapsed where they were. At the last moment, the third wasp changed position, and the arrow glanced off the remaining insect's hard head! The wasp spread its wings and launched into the air, but its speed was no match for the fourth arrow.

The captain, sighting along his arrow's shaft, fired the instant he realized the other arrow missed its target. His arrow flashed across the field and was embedded with a thud into the body of the wasp. The insect didn't get more than six feet off the ground. The captain moved his thumb to the back of the bow and pressed a button. Instantly the wasp went stiff as the electric shock arched through its body. It dropped to the ground with a loud thump, and a cloud of dust swirled into the air.

There was silence for a moment, then, "Ranger one to second squad, advance and confirm the kills!"

The second squad, arrows ready, approached the center of the field. "Kills confirmed, Cap."

"Ranger one to Ranger team, great job guys. Fall out, and get this mess cleaned up."

Then there was a shout of joy from all the rangers!

"Ranger one to command center, sound the all clear!"

"Yes, sir" was the reply.

And a moment later the siren could be heard once more in the distance.

It didn't take long for the rangers to pile the dead wasps onto the flatbed truck and strap them down.

"Ranger one to squad, leaders two and four meet me by the truck!"

In a few moments the two squad leaders reported to the captain. "Eric, I need you to take second squad to the outer perimeter and find the breech! Bryan, you do the same with the forth squad on the inner perimeter! We have got to find out how they got in! I want thirty-minute com. Check with the control center, and as soon as the opening is located, we will send out a repair crew. Stay on station until the repairs are completed."

"Yes, sir."

With their new orders, the leaders were off to gather their squads and head out.

Over the com link the captain announced, "Everybody on your toes and remember this is a big day. We have some very special guest coming this afternoon, so look sharp. We don't want any more intruders today!"

Later that day…

Eric had reported the breach repaired, and the squad was returning to the compound. Bryan had just reported to the captain and his team had gone to the dining hall to get some lunch. Just then the truck with second squad pulled into the compound. Eric jumped out and came over to where the captain was standing.

"Well, did you find where the wasps got in?" asked the captain.

"Yes, sir! One of the double-door hatches had come loose, and they had managed to pry it open. I have the maintenance team along with my squad going over every one of the hatches now, and so far they have found everything is okay!" Eric answered.

"How long will it take to complete their inspection?"

"They will be done way before our guests arrive," Eric said, and then he continued, "So there's plenty of time for me to polish your brass, clean your boots, and press your pants, Your Lordship!" he said with a laugh.

"Now cut that out, Eric, you know I still think you should be the captain, not me! Michael replied.

Eric was laughing so hard at Michael's red face that he was doubled over.

"Not me!" Eric exclaimed. "You're older than me, remember. Besides, now you get to worry about inspections and intruders and all that. I just have my squad to worry about!"

"Well, next year when you can take over, I get to sit back and watch you worry!" Michael said.

Mike and Eric had become the best of friends after working together in Ireland and now here in Tennessee.

The responsibility of keeping the town secure and its residences safe had fallen on the two of them. Once the Irish Tinys arrived and the additional housing was built, their quaint little village soon became a thriving settlement. Working together, they had combined the scouts from America and the hunters from Ireland into a unit that was patterned after the old Texas Rangers. With a captain that was the leader of the group, squads, and squad leaders, Michael had been voted in as their first captain.

"Okay, go ahead and get something to eat and then get back to whatever you were doing to get ready for our guest!" Michael said.

"Yes, my captain!" Eric smirked with a deep bow, and as he turned to leave, he jumped to one side just in time to make Mike's kick at his behind miss.

"Ha, ha! Missed again," Eric taunted as he ran off to the dining hall.

Later that same day, the guests began arriving at Grandpa's house for the special celebration.

Conor, Brittany and Katelyn had driven in the night before. Scott and Janet were due anytime now; Ed and Heather was just pulling in to park, at the front of the house, when Conor's cell phone rang. He and Grandpa were sitting at the kitchen table having coffee. He pulled it out of his pocket and saw that he had a text message. Flipping open the phone, he read, "Just turned into the driveway."

Grandpa looked at him with concern, "Anything wrong, Grandson?"

"Nope, it's from Scott, they're on the driveway. Should be here in about three minutes if they don't fall into one of those ruts and disappear!" Conor remarked, and they both laughed.

"Grandpa, are you ever going to have those ruts repaired and the driveway paved?" Conor asked.

"Nope! Those ruts are a great deterrent to looky loos and noisy people. They stay! And besides, Grandma and I only go to town about once a month. We're never in a big hurry like you youngins are."

Just then Ed and Heather came in. "Good morning, everyone!" they said as they came over and sat down at the table with Conor and Grandpa. "How's everyone today?"

Grandpa smiled and answered, "If we were any more blessed, we'd have to be in heaven! And how are you?"

"I'm okay! Looking forward to today's gathering," Ed replied and then stopped to think for a minute before saying, "You know, I have never seen the Tinys' village!"

"Well, we can fix that just as soon as the rest of the guests arrive."

Grandma and Katelyn came into the kitchen. When they saw Ed and Heather, they both came over and gave them hugs.

"Would you like some coffee or tea?" Katelyn asked even before Grandma could get her mouth open.

"Coffee would be great," Ed said.

Heather asked, "I don't want to be a bother, but could I get a spot of tea?"

Grandma watched as Katelyn went over to the cabinet, got a cups, removed the pot from the coffee maker, poured Ed a cup, and gave it to him. Then she put on a pot of water for tea. Grandma smiled and was very pleased that Katelyn felt so comfortable in their home. *That's a good sign,* she thought to herself.

Finally, Scott and Janet arrived and were greeted with hugs and handshakes all around.

Scott announced, "Well, is everyone ready to go see our handy work?"

"Yes!" everyone responded.

All of them headed out the back door and into the woods. They traveled the same path that Conor, Brittany and Janet took so many months ago when they first met all the Tennessee Tinys. Now they were going to see all the Tinys together, at last!

After they had traveled for a little over a quarter of a mile, they came to the same rocks that Grandpa had used to open the sticker bushes before. He did the honors again, and in they went.

Conor stepped forward and called out in the direction of the line of trees. "Okay, Michael, show yourselves."

With that, all of a sudden around the largest of the trees appeared what looked like a glass dome. Conor turned to the group and said, "Welcome to *Free-Dome*!"

Inside the dome everyone could now see the Tinys smiling and waving up at their friends.

This time it was Ed that said, "Wow! That was impressive, Scott, nice work! Graybeard, Eric, and Michael along with Shawn Dugan came out of the dome to greet the group. They

all went over to the far side of the clearing where Grandpa had placed a picnic table and benches, so the big people would have a place to sit when they visited. After they have all exchanged their greetings, Janet asked, "Well, Mr. Dugan, what do you and our Irish friends think of all this?"

The Tinys were all sitting on the table and the group of Bigs on the benches on either side.

Shawn looked over at Janet and answered, "Me name's Shawn, lass, not Mr. Dugan." He said with a big grin on his face, "And we thank the Lord for all of you and this marvelous contraption that Scott and Conor have made to keep us all safe here in beautiful Tennessee!"

Grandpa and Grandma looked at each other then around at this group, made up of big and little people, gathered here. Finally, they felt that their Tiny friends would be well cared for and safe.